"Kate!" Angie lifted herself onto one elbow and gave Kate an impish grin. "Will you marry me?"

"What?" Kate laughed in relief. At least it was evident from the question that Angie wasn't rejecting her.

"Kate, I'm not into a one night stand. And I'm not sure where you're at with this. So we make love now, and then what? This afternoon at the barbecue you avert your eyes when I look at you. Next week you transfer me into another department at work. All because you're embarrassed over something that shouldn't have happened. I want you for more than a morning. Your friendship matters to me. I want you to go now, because I want you to come back later, when you've thought about it, and give me what I need — if you can do that. If you don't come back, then we still have our friendship. Understand, sweetheart? I'm not dismissing you. I love you just as much either way."

Strength resided in the possibility of her body as it rested momentarily on Angie's; in the perfection of her power as she surrendered it to another woman. For a fleeting instant she knew that power thus given is power recycled, magnified, returned. Kate held her breath, rested her head on Angie's breast. She felt in her body, within the circle of another's arms, the liberation of a runner for whom time and space explode through infinity, and the spirit surges like a newly created universe. This was freedom. She would be back.

Sunday's Child
by Joyce Bright

Naiad Press, Inc.
1988

Printed in the United States of America
First Edition

Edited by Katherine V. Forrest
Cover design by The Women's Graphic Center
Typesetting by Sandi Stancil

Library of Congress Cataloging-in-Publication Data

Bright, Joyce 1947—
    Sunday's child / Joyce Bright.
    p.   cm.
    ISBN 0-941483-12-6 : $8.95
    I. Title
PS3552.R4627S8   1988   87-31189
813'.54--dc 19   CIP

Dedication

To Judith who in death reminds me daily of how important we are to each other; to Gail who teaches me the importance of extended family; to Katherine who is patiently nurturing and Linda who intuitively counsels and Bobbie who fixes things and Connie who does art and Rosanna who believes in miracles and Peggy who has courage and Jill who cares very much and Jodi who throws the javelin and Denny who is honest; to all women who in friendship and in love through their wisdom and diverse talents make powerful each other and our community.

About the Author

The author has reviewed books and written articles for the gay press for the last ten years. She worked as a hospital clerk for 20 years before becoming the office manager of the Sacramento Rape Crisis Center. Currently she works in AIDS education. She has a degree in philosophy, and is presently completing a master's degree in counseling.

Chapter 1

The May morning had a sliver of crispness to it, an edge of freshness and promise. Kate Ashbourne, in her running shorts, stood tapping on the apartment door. Sweat dripped down her forehead as goose bumps broke out on her long muscular legs. She smiled inwardly, happy with the day.

"Come on Angie," she addressed the door. As she tapped more urgently the clear jabs of noise perforated the thin air. She heard footsteps, then the curtains receded just enough to allow two large gray-blue eyes a first squinting view of the day.

The door flew open. "Kate! What's the matter? What's wrong?"

Angie Mandelli, all five foot-seven inches of her, stood naked, her brown nipples erect, her short black hair jutting in all directions. With the pounce of a mongoose she grabbed Kate's arm and swung her into the apartment. "What's happened?"

"Nothing's wrong." Seeing her friend in such disarray, Kate chuckled. She knew she would pay for this later. "I came by to get you to go running. Put on your shorts, sweetie, and let's go." Kate's matter-of-fact staccato contrasted sharply with the nervous run-on of Angie's whiskey tones.

Angie, who stood intensely concentrating two inches from Kate's nose, loosened her grip on Kate's arm. Glaring into Kate's pale green eyes, she pinched her shoulders in disbelief, threw her arms out in despair, and walked from the room.

"If nothing's wrong with Kate," Angie mumbled to herself in the bedroom, "then clearly something's the matter with me." Kate was like a sister and that carried certain privileges. But a 6:30 wake-up on Saturday morning — with no apparent emergency — *that* stretched the limits of sisterhood. Especially, Angie noted as she reached under the bed for her running shoes, when Rochelle lay so invitingly on the double bed.

Rochelle, of course, could sleep through thunderous knocks on the door, Angie's mumbling, and probably a personal visit from the River Rapist. From the sirens at three this morning, the rapist had hit the neighborhood again last night. That made it twice this month. Coming home early that Saturday morning three weeks ago, Angie had counted twelve patrol cars. Christ! Her stomach churned and her thoughts returned to Rochelle. Rochelle never slept through light kisses on her neck or fingertip caresses down her back. Like a cat, the woman had her priorities. Angie moaned inwardly and, carrying her running shoes, returned to the living room.

While Angie sat on the living room floor tying her shoes, Kate surveyed the neat arrangement of Angie's antique furniture, her eyes finally coming to rest on the oriental silk screen by the fireplace. She sighed, apprehensive over Angie's silence. Well, she had never seen Angie at this hour of the day. Usually they ran at 7:30, before work on weekdays. In the winter they occasionally went out after work. Angie was good for five or six miles, no more. On her longer runs, Kate ran alone or with Alex who biked while she ran.

"Have to leave Rochelle a note. She'll wonder where I am when she wakes up." Angie knew Rochelle would still be in bed when she returned but she wanted to alert Kate to the sacrifice she was making, instill a little guilt. She got up and bounded into the kitchen.

Kate smiled at Angie's energy. Angie met the world with zest, with strong impulse, with a directness that suggested life was clear and comprehensible. Kate admired that in Angie, admired the freedom of her gestures, the lack of self-consciousness in her face and in her body. Kate compared herself to Angie, compared her English reticence to Angie's Italian passion, and although she didn't feel jealous, she momentarily cursed her parents and her profession. *Reading X rays all day in front of a viewing box is both too cerebral and too isolating. I need something else!* Her thoughts returned to Angie as a projection of hope, as a fantasy of happy times. Angie was the most beautiful present under the Christmas tree.

"Let's go." Angie walked out the front door and Kate followed, making sure the door locked as she closed it.

"Aren't you going to stretch?" Kate asked.

"Why? My body won't know it's up for another hour."

"You're trying to punish me, right? Make me feel guilty?"

"Kate." Angie struck a compromise tone between truth and tease. "You're inured to guilt or you wouldn't be here. I only hope on ever so minimal a level to impart some sense of social reciprocity in you so that at a later date — when I'm in need . . ."

"Yes?"

"You'll remember all I've done for you."

"Ah ha." Kate bent from the waist, touching her toes. "You'll thank me for this later."

"That's what God said just before the flood." Angie, following Kate's lead, touched her toes.

Waking up gradually, Angie appraised the flexible, fluid lines of Kate's legs. Well, she thought, maybe Kate had fifteen pounds on her, but it was all taken up in smooth lines. If her parents had given her ballet lessons, she'd have Kate's flexibility. Or maybe she'd only have knottier muscles.

"Not so hard," Kate gently cautioned.

"Pul-lease, Kate. It's too early for conversation."

Kate threw back her head, and the morning's pleasure came through in an easy laugh. She shook her head at Angie. "Sweetie, I doubt your mouth observes any curfew."

Angie laughed too, her smile flowing up through her eyes. She tossed Kate an up-your-ass gesture, rumpled Kate's hair. "Let's go."

They cut the blue morning air with graceful strides. The deserted county back roads, protecting somnolent

4

houses, accepted without notice their synchronized breathing and steady eight minute mile pace. They ran for fifteen minutes, silent, renewing their solidarity through shared exertion.

"Why does my friend have to be a superjock?" Angie panted.

"I am not a superjock," Kate replied defensively, then laughed to cover her defensiveness. Accustomed to a faster pace, this run was a slow jog for her. Reversing their normal conversational patterns, Kate did most of the talking when they ran, and Angie, usually loquacious, concentrated on conserving her energy.

"National eight hundred meter champ —" Angie's voice carried pride.

"Exactly twenty-four years ago, Angie. My last year of high school. The glory days are long gone."

"Qualified for the Olympics."

"And didn't make it," Kate finished.

The finality of Kate's tone caught Angie by surprise. She tried to feel her way around this subject: "You broke an arm."

"Diabolical of me, don't you think?" Kate didn't wait for an answer. "I've had twenty-four years to wonder over that arm. I'm not sure I believe in accidents."

"Right." Angie's response was noncommittal. She puzzled over Kate's terse tone. Now that she thought of it, Alex had been the one to tell her about Kate's national ranking. Kate had never mentioned it.

"You probably wish I'd done permanent damage to my right femur — so I wouldn't pound at your door at six-thirty on a Saturday morning, right?" Kate's voice had returned to normal. She punched Angie playfully.

Angie countered in her best Italian godfather imitation, "Don'a mess with this muscle, woman." Not understanding Kate's refusal to talk about the Olympics, she nevertheless allowed the subject to drop.

But as they ran on in silence, Angie did not drop the subject from her thoughts. She understood the nature of reticence only by way of her sexual orientation which she had discovered at an early age. Sanding barefoot in the kitchen, twelve years old, she told her mother she liked girls. Mama frowned, always a bad sign. "Washa you face, Lena. We talk later." Although Mama called her Lena, an endearment shortened from Angelina, her manner meant this subject was closed forever. Yet normally in the constellation of her large family, reticence only insured that you did not shine; reserve diminished your star. The Olympics was not something about which any member of her family would be humble.

Kate interrupted Angie's thoughts. "I've been thinking about competing again."

This is it, Angie told herself, her intuition in full play. "Whadaya mean? The Olympics?"

"Angelina! You're a mind reader. How did you know?"

"*Ave Maria.*" Angie raised her arms and face to the sky, and waited for an explanation.

"I want to qualify for the Olympic trials in the marathon." Kate held up a hand before Angie could cut in. "Qualifying time for the trials is only 2:53."

"A piece of cake." Angie, missing a stride, looked incredulously at her friend. Her immediate inclination was to stop running, to go home and, over a cup of coffee, discuss this in depth. Instead she slowed the pace. "So you're going to run twenty-six miles in two hours and fifty-three minutes. Why not? We put people on the moon."

"You don't think I can do it?" Kate momentarily wanted to hit her. This was her punishment for getting Angie up so early.

Angie touched her reassuringly on the shoulder. "Why do you *want* to do it? Can you be competitive in the Olympics?"

"No, no. It's the trials I want to qualify for. I want to run in the trials! Only the top three from the trials go on to the Olympics, and I couldn't make that cut. But the best women in the country get invited to the trials. I want to run with the best one more time."

"I'm not enough for you, huh?" Angie smiled. "No one's ever told me that before, Katie."

Kate laughed at her. "Oh, be quiet and listen. I ran the Sacramento International Marathon last year in three hours and eleven minutes. But this is the thing — I didn't have to work hard for it. It was easy."

Angie looked at her skeptically, and did some quick calculations. "You'll need to take off nearly a minute a mile. That's a lot!"

"I don't think so." Kate was confident. "With some help, with proper training. I mean *real* training. The Sacramento International Marathon is coming up in December again, and lots of class runners will be using it to qualify for the Olympics. It's one of the last qualifying marathons. It's flat. The weather's perfect. Cold. Sometimes wet. The trials are in Eugene in May, a year from now."

Angie deflected the subject. "How long have we been running?" As Kate had grown excited about her marathon, she had also picked up the pace so that now all Angie could concentrate on was her labored breathing.

7

"About twenty-five minutes. You're doing great! Want to go for seven miles this morning?"

Angie shot her a glance.

"Sorry. Guess I picked up the pace on you." Kate looked at her watch. "We must have done that last mile in 7:20. Good for you, Angie."

They turned back. Although Angie wasn't up to admitting it, she felt great and was glad Kate had come by. She loved running in this area; its country setting reminded her of her Mendocino childhood. Racing through forests, herding cows at her aunt's ranch, playing hide-and-go-seek with cousins — running was freedom and innocence. Now it was also the vanity of a woman not ready to grow old. She smiled inside.

These winding, narrow residential roads they ran on had been around for thirty years or more. The homes, ranch style or California Spanish, sat back from the lanes. Stables and tennis courts attested to leisure priorities. They ran by two maple trees, the scent filling Angie's head with attending images of pancakes and bacon. A Great Dane came running up to them; but the women knew all the dogs in the neighborhood, and this particular Dane was friendly, only wanted to run with them for a while. Thirty foot twin pines came into view and Angie knew they had two miles to go.

"So about the Olympics," Kate continued, having given her friend some breathing space. Mentally she tensed, and then plunged in as directly as her nature allowed: "I need to do some weight training for upper body strength. A whirlpool would be nice on these joints —"

"A hot tub. You're getting a hot tub!"

"Not exactly. I'm asking you to join a health club with me."

"What?" Angie slowed to a walk, and tugged on Kate's sleeve. "Katie, I set trends! I do not follow them. Ask Jodi at main reception. She not only follows trends, she *needs* a health spa."

"Now, sweetie." Kate clenched her jaw, and pulled Angie forward, willing her to run. Angie fell back into pace.

This was going to be as difficult as Kate had imagined. She knew a health club would offend Angie's sense of style, but Angie was her best friend. Moreover, if she could only get Angie's agreement, she knew Angie could be counted on. Angie always did as she promised, and she did it with intensity. A perfect coach. She gave no slack.

"No." Angie paused and then continued, "Weights? Dammit! You *are* a jock."

"You're a lesbian." Maybe she could appeal to Angie's feminism and sense of esthetics, Kate reasoned. Angie did work on the rape-crisis hot-line, and she had heard Angie talk about self-defense classes they held down at the rape crisis center. Surely lifting weights was politically correct.

"Katie." Angie stopped running again, totally thrown off balance by this latest argument. "I'm not ready to come out to the entire neighborhood before breakfast," she whispered. "Keep your voice down."

"Sorry." Kate hung her head, confused. Since when was Angie shy about being a lesbian?

"Besides," Angie continued to whisper, "whatever do you think we do in bed? Honey, I don't know what misshapen stereotype you're carrying around in that brilliant head of yours, but my bed is not a weight bench. 'Bench press your way to lesbian fulfillment' is not something I've ever seen on a poster at the Gay Parade. It's breast, not pecs, that turn me on —"

9

"Hush." Kate laughed and held up her hand. "Don't you have an Amazon ideal? You know, a complete physical woman?"

Angie thought for a moment. "I'm pretty sure that's politically incorrect, Kate. I'm certain we're not supposed to pick women based on their muscle tone. The idea is that you get to know another woman based on her heart and mind, and then the physical just flows — no matter what the woman looks like." Angie smiled knowingly to herself and then giggled out loud. "Well, God knows, theory and practice have never been a good match."

"Angie." Kate was getting impatient. "Aside from politics, what do you think personally?"

"What? You think at thirty-eight I can become an Amazon?" Angie scoffed. "Nah. I don't think so," she offered after brief consideration. But even as she voiced this disclaimer, the idea suddenly appealed to her. She looked down at her biceps.

"Sure!" Kate offered in her most enthusiastic voice, not at all sure that she could picture Angie as an Amazon. She had meant only to tempt her with the concept, but if that was politically incorrect then making Angie over would do. "Why in six months to a year we could change our whole physical appearance. Lean and mean, Angie. Think of it." Kate started running again, and Angie followed.

"We're too old." Angie looked at her friend seriously, and frowned.

"We are not!" Kate knew she had Angie hooked. She felt it, and that gave her courage to continue: "Besides, I need you. I'm not sure I can do this alone. You're my best friend."

"Can't I just wave pompoms as you drive off to the gym?" Kate seldom made emotional appeals. Angie felt herself capitulate. She couldn't refuse a clear statement of need, but maybe she could negotiate lesser involvement. "What about Alex? He's your lover."

"Alex's hours are too erratic. I know he's only a podiatrist but he still has house rounds at the hospital and sometimes he doesn't get away until seven or eight."

"Dammit, Katie! Stop running! I can't breathe and think at the same time! Now what exactly is this about?" Kate slowed to walk beside her. "Why the Olympic trials?

Kate took a deep breath. How to explain to Angie what she couldn't explain to herself? She felt herself grow nervous — she hated these kinds of conversations. Maybe she *was* a jock — all her heroes, with the exception of Angie who after all was a friend, were women who endured pain silently, who dropped on the track and joked in the locker room. These women did not complain. Maybe, Kate reflected, maybe she really didn't have what it takes.

"It seems worthwhile," Kate started. "I'm forty-two. I'm not going to have children. Hell, I can't even decide whether to marry Alex. He's ten years younger and sometimes I feel so tired and old next to him. I need to risk something. Angie, I need to have something at stake. Sports are real to me. They represent clean endeavor, purity of focus. I need to win at something that is meaningful to me. God, Angie —" Kate turned to her. "When I run, when I run fast and strong — then I feel alive. The rest of the time I feel like an imposter. I'm scared. I'm bored. I need the real physical pain of running — I need the Olympic trials." Kate pounded the last sentence out rhythmically.

Silence fell between them, and then Kate whispered, "I feel time . . . and my motivation for living slipping away. Running is the only way I know to find myself. The

Olympic trials are the only way the universe has of telling me I'm good enough to go on."

Touched, Angie didn't know how to respond. She hadn't known Kate was considering marriage to Alex. Kate, in her eyes, was far from being a tired old woman; she was an existential heroine, a powerful woman with grace and warmth who cut her own path. Having no greater ambition than to write a solid history book, Angie had a hard time understanding either Kate's sense of competitiveness or her need to excel. But if she couldn't understand Kate's motive, she did feel the truth of Kate's emotions and trusted the integrity of Kate's own way of knowing. That was enough. What Kate needed, Kate would have.

"Katie!" Angie exploded with the full resonance of her voice. "Let's go for it! The Olympic trials, lady!"

Kate, her strawberry blonde hair falling out of its bun and sticking to the nape of her neck, reached across the two feet that separated them, and hugged Angie.

Angie laughed. "Lean and mean, huh?"

Angie walked into the apartment. Jolted by the distinct scent of fresh coffee, she followed her nose into the kitchen, and reached for her mug, already filled with hot water to preheat it.

"A good run, beautiful?" Rochelle's voice always teased.

Angie turned. Rochelle's small body — a size three, Angie knew — advanced toward her, naked except for gold chains. Angie gathered all her powers of resistance to answer Rochelle's question. Why was it that conversation was always so minimal between them?

"The run was fine." Angie smiled as Rochelle walked into her arms, snuggled under her chin. "But Kate —"

Rochelle's almond shaped blue eyes looked into Angie's face. "You're all wet." It was a simple statement.

"Yes." Angie nodded slowly, and raised an eyebrow.

Rochelle licked at the sweat on Angie's neck, and felt underneath Angie's T-shirt. "You smell delicious, darling."

Angie sighed, and lifted Rochelle's mouth to her own. This was why their conversation was minimal, she reminded herself helplessly.

Chapter 2

On Monday morning two weeks later, Angie, pulling off her linen jacket, whirled into what was known as the hospital reading room. She pirouetted on a two-inch beige heel, plunged into a desk chair, and glared at the back of Kate who sat dictating X ray reports into a recorder.

Obviously a glare would not get Kate's attention. Angie sighed loudly. "Two weeks to get a gun in this town!" The announcement was greeted by Kate's unmoving back. "Two damn weeks. For chrissake, I'm not ordering a Thanksgiving turkey."

"Too late for that, sweetie," Kate replied calmly. Angie's non sequiturs invariably hooked Kate's logically trained mind. "This being the end of May here in Poland we all have our turkey orders in."

"Kate, they don't celebrate Thanksgiving in Poland." Angie stood, placed her jacket on a hook, and removed a white lab coat form the coat stand. "My life's at stake and you're joking," she noted flatly. Then: "These lab coats are simply not Christian Dior."

Kate turned off her recorder, swiveled in her chair, and faced Angie. "My, aren't we spiffy this morning. Let me see that jacket. Nice. Linen?"

"Irish linen." Angie nodded proudly and put the jacket on for Kate. "The best. Ralph Lauren."

"Ah hah. Do you know any other designer? You're forty-five minutes late because you've been looking for a gun to complete this classic ensemble. As accessories go, sweetie, I think a gun would be a bit much but then —"

"*Un momento.*" Angie held up both hands. "A psychopathic rapist swaggers at will through my neighborhood — my neighborhood! — and you reprimand me for forty-five minutes. We are concerned here with the rest of my life. We're talking about to be or not to be, Katie." Controlled hysteria charged Angie's voice. "Bye bye Lena, my mother's child gone forever! You're insensitive — and I agreed to work out at a gym with you. Gratitude." Angie shook her head sadly.

Trying not to smile, Kate stitched her blonde eyebrows together, and considered which end of this outburst to address. Why was it that Angie could wear wrinkled linen and still look fresh? Probably her straight lines and healthy complexion. Her body was made for designer clothes.

"Your mama would drop in a terminal faint if she even vaguely suspected her daughter of toting a gun. What is this? Why do you think the River Rapist is after you personally?" Kate held up a long, manicured hand to prevent Angie from answering. "He doesn't seem to care if men or women are in the house. Therefore, it's not because you're single." As an afterthought: "Rochelle is there often enough anyway. Now, have you received a message from this man to the effect that he wants you specifically? No," she answered her own question. "As you well know, in certain circles your attitude would be considered paranoid." Kate rested her case.

Momentarily stunned into silence, Angie stared into Kate's eyes. "Christ, let me get ahold of myself here. You think I'm par-a-noid?" She flung a hand to her breast. "Surely, Kate, you're aware of the laws of total randomness. I'm living in a determined mathematical envelope. This man struck again Friday night, not three blocks from my house. Don't you realize that my exact apartment could well coincide with this man's chaotic spikes?"

"*What* are you talking about, child?" Kate wasn't sure if Angie was interpreting some new UCLA research study or spouting New Age gibberish. She was capable of either.

"Kate, consciousness is the arbiter of randomness. And my particular consciousness is aware that a single-cell amoeba in seeming randomness becomes a slime mold covering an entire lake. With a head and a tail and a billion cells. Did you know that?"

"I'm speechless," Kate deadpanned.

"The police chased him through a field, down to the river. He had to pass not half a foot from my patio. Had I been there —" Angie pointed to her chest with a nicely filed index finger — "I could have heard him pant as he whizzed by. Now tell me, Katie — paranoid? He's made fools of the police. Raped half of Sacramento —"

"Thirteen."

"What?" Kate didn't always make sense to Angie.

"He's raped thirteen women. I didn't say only thirteen. In five months thirteen rapes are outrageous. However, that is not legion. As for the boys in blue, they do as well as their fear, intelligence, and public cooperation will allow."

"Oh, batshit! They drink Coors, watch sit-coms on the boob tube, and plunder our dwindling wilderness with dirt bikes. Every male is not your protector, you know."

Like a broken blood vessel, rage exploded in Kate's brain, and her mind went momentarily blank. She shook her head. She was suddenly so angry with Angie she wanted to walk out of the room. "I know not every male is my protector, Mandelli," she muttered through a clenched jaw and frozen smile. "On the other hand, not every rapist is after your skinny body."

"I know that," Angie bridled, her own temper suddenly rising. She felt confused. A memory, like a forgotten name, nudged at her.

"Now I grant you the idea of rape is hideous, but it is not death." Kate's rational mind had returned. "And he has not killed anyone yet."

"Yet," Angie replied skeptically. "Listen, you can't even buy a deadbolt in this city."

"Angie," Kate interrupted. "You're a rape crisis advocate, and I remember you talking about a commitment to non-violence. What's this thing about a gun?"

"I took myself off the crisis line, Kate. I had to. In one six hour shift last month I received twelve calls. It's crazy

17

out there. And the calls just feed my own fear. I'm no good as a counselor right now."

"But what about the commitment to non-violence?" It finally struck her that Angie was dead serious about this.

"Katie, there are only a few patterns of resistance against the stress of circumstances —"

"Situational ethics, Gandhi?"

"I'm not proud of this." Angie hung her head. "I'm scared! Everyone out there is scared. Why not you? Have you ever been raped?"

"Have you?" Kate shot back quickly.

Angie decided to avoid Kate's question. "Oh, Kate, what am I going to do?" Of course she hadn't been raped — nor had Kate. Rape happened to other women, the women she cared for on the crisis line.

Kate said, "I've told you more than once you're welcome to stay in the cottage behind my house. If my brother weren't staying in the house you could have the upstairs bedroom. God knows the house is big enough for all of us, but Scott probably wouldn't understand you sleeping in my bed for an indefinite period of time. He raises an eyebrow when Alex spends the night. I mean, he adores you, of course . . ."

"But he might suddenly think you'd become a little bit lesbian. I understand, Kate, homophobia happens in the best of families." Angie was smiling; she liked Scott.

"What do you do when you have a prude for a brother?"

"You're asking me? My brother's a monsignor. You pray that their souls don't become as shriveled as their genitalia." Angie caught Kate's raised eyebrow, and quickly added, "I'm joking."

"The fact that you can at a moment like this indicates you're basically sane." Kate nodded.

"Of course." Angie returned to Kate's offer. "The rapist is working his way into your area. A little further away from the river. Remember that woman who came into ER last week? Her mind will never be the same. He's a sadist, you know."

"Speaking of ER, Mrs. Buck was in again last night. Would you be so kind as to find her old X rays so I can compare this new chest?"

"Buck's a hypochondriac; she's going to die of radiation poisoning." Angie sighed and walked over to Kate to get Buck's medical record number. "You don't care about me or my real fears. That's OK. I'm stable." Angie bent over Kate and copied the number. Kate smelled good to her. "My life hangs by a small thread, and you want me to go in search of X rays. No problem."

"Angie, why don't you spend the night? You're all worked up." Kate, as was her inclination with most people she liked, placed an arm around Angie's waist. "We'll go over to your place after work and pick up some clothes. Go out to dinner. Did you get in any running this weekend?"

Quickly Angie ran a hand down Kate's shoulder. "Three miles yesterday at the track. Fast. I'm sure it would have been faster if I'd gone to the gun shop first." She groaned and repeated, "Two weeks to get a gun."

"Why don't we think of a new place to eat? At any rate, I promise to keep the rapist away while you sleep."

"Oh, you know how you are about your privacy. Even Alex gets on your nerves."

It was true, Angie reflected. After knowing Kate for five years she still did not know her private world well. She attributed that to heterosexual superficiality: Straight people carried their private lives around like reefs warding off the ocean. Only their close relatives had

19

the benefit of private drama. Lesbians, on the other hand, carried their private lives like a stage upon which to launch a public performance. No secrets in lesbianland. Of course, Angie corrected, lesbianland was one big family.

"Let me see if I have this right," Kate interrupted Angie's thoughts. "You're more concerned with my privacy than with your life — which you assure me is at stake here. Is that right?"

Angie nodded. "I'm considerate."

Kate smiled, charmed as always by both Angie's feigned innocence and her conceit. "Girl, you don't have a healthy sense of survival. But I won't beg. Think about it. In the meantime, I don't want to hear another word about the rapist. Get me my X rays, sweetie."

Kate turned her back to her desk and its X ray viewing boxes. As she switched on the dictating recorder she heard Angie leave the room. She smiled to herself as she studied the films before her and continued dictating:

PORTABLE CHEST: PA and lateral views reveal the heart and mediastinum to be within normal limits. No evidence of congestive failure is seen. IMPRESSION: No active disease noted.

The telephone rang. It was Don Sutherland, one of the cardiologists and a favorite friend of Alex. Don flirted with abandon and had made it clear that he would gladly sacrifice Alex's friendship for Kate's body. Why, Kate wondered, did otherwise sensitive and good doctors have to be such social and moral morons?

He was concerned about a patient's chest film. Kate flattered him: "A nice job you did on that Swan-Ganz catheter. The right lung is totally clear. Nothing to worry about."

"So who's worried? How about lunch today?"

"I'm meeting Alex."

"Someday you'll be in urgent need of a great open heart surgeon, and there you'll be stuck in the arms of a lowly podiatrist. Then what?"

"My feet will look good as they wheel me into surgery."

"Sure. Say, you want to join Alex and me for a beer after work?"

"I'm busy, Don." As she eased him off the phone, she suddenly felt sorry for him. At a dinner last Friday night he had looked ghastly — white and tired and tense. When he had left the party early, glances of concern followed him. Kate knew that doctors understood tiredness like athletes knew pain — you carried it constantly without paying much attention to it. But perhaps something was wrong with Don.

Kate took the films she had been reading off the viewing box and returned them to their X ray jacket. Snapping Mabel Win's chest films into the box, she sat back, wished for a cup of coffee, and dictated:

CHEST: There is a nodular area, 1–2 cm. in diameter with poor margins in the left apex. This nodular lesion has been present without definite change dating back to the first film available in this department 3-28-83. Its appearance changes slightly from film to film, but it is not definitely enlarging when compared to two months ago. This could still be a slow growing peripheral neoplasm, but its relative stability over several months suggests that it might be a parenchymal scar or an inactive granuloma. The heart is not enlarged and the lungs are otherwise clear. CONCLUSION:

Ill-defined 1–2 cm. nodular lesion in the left apex present for six months without change.

Kate pulled the films off the viewing box. She switched off the dictating machine as Angie, X rays tucked under her arm, came back into the room. Frank Blair was five paces behind her.

"Ashbourne," he ordered, "look at these films and tell me if what you see is what I see."

With a good deal of diffidence Kate placed the films on her viewing box. As she slowly examined the chest films she resisted the desire to ask Angie to get some coffee. She muffled a yawn.

"The vascular markings appear to be increased. Here," she pointed. "Pulmonary vascular congestion, possibly with some edema in the perivascular interstitial space. Some edema of the interlobular septa. See? No enlargement of the heart. Fluid overload I would say. What did you see, Frank?"

"Same thing." He glared at her, turned, and marched from the room.

"God, that man's an ass. His secretary used to be a nice woman. Now Jennifer's as bad as he is," Angie gossiped. "Here's Buck's old and new chest. You know I can read this one. Out of my way, Ashbourne."

Angie shoved the 11×17 films under the clips on the viewing box. "Ah ha, just as I thought. Normal heart size. Lungs and pleural spaces appear clear. Impression: Negative chest." She turned to Kate and smiled.

The smile opened Kate's heart as cleanly as a scalpel. This thirty-eight-year-old woman was her child. "Practicing without a license. I'll have to report you to the AMA. But your reading was perfect. Especially since you had the lateral upside-down."

"A talent they envied in my medical class," Angie said, giggling. "Just before I dropped out. Died of terminal boredom, don't ya know. But the secret is in my dyslexia."

"Ah ha. I had no idea. Listen, why don't you go get us some coffee or — you can read this IVP and I'll get us some coffee."

"I only do chests; I'm a specialist." Angie held up her hand in protest. "I could never pollute my eyes with all that tangle of bowels. It's obscene, Katie. I'll get the coffee, maybe talk with some friends. Be back in thirty or forty minutes."

"Of course. Having put in a good ten or twenty minutes this morning, I guess that's fair. Maybe a nap when you return." Kate reached into her purse for change. "You know, you probably missed your calling. With all your hot air, God only knows what you could do with intestinal gas patterns."

"Not me." Angie laughed. "Writing history is *my* love. I clerk at this hospital simply for the surreal high of it all. Why, I get a contact high just walking into some corridors. Syringes are passed out when you walk into any number of departments. You know the clerk's motto: 'Better living through chemistry.' "

"Go. Coffee." Kate pointed to the door and pushed Angie. As Angie left the room, Kate shook her head thinking back on the time two years ago when Angie had gotten her involved in the hospital campaign to eliminate drugs from the work place. Three people in housekeeping had been arrested for selling drugs, several workers had been brought into a drug rehabilitation project; but in general the campaign had just slowly petered out. When the doctors prescribed less medications, the working staff found drugs elsewhere, and the administrators pondered the legal ramifications of spot drug testing.

Kate preferred to think of Angie's writing. She had difficulty visualizing Angie concentrating silently over books in a public library. Yet she had read some of Angie's work: historical pieces on the Victorian homes downtown, articles she had done for *Modern California Living* or the gay presses. Angie took her writing seriously, and Kate respected that, having herself a love for the written word. Kate sighed. It seemed like a thousand years ago when she had received her undergraduate degree in the humanities. Or had it been only yesterday and her body, aging in a vacuum of time, defied laws not yet written?

Angie dashed for the cafeteria. She rushed everywhere, giving the impression that she was one busy clerk. Yet her job barely required four hours of work a day, and much of that was spent socializing.

For the last three years she had been the hospital reading room clerk. It was her job to match new films with the pertinent old films when emergency room patients or hospital patients had X rays taken, so that Kate would have both sets of films available for comparison. Twice a day Angie went to ER to pick up films on new hospital admits. She retrieved their old films, if there were any, in the hospital file room, and organized all the films for Kate and the attending doctors. A three-hundred bed hospital required that kind of clerk — but not for eight hours a day. In fact, this part of her job barely required two hours.

In the afternoon she walked around to all the hospital stations and picked up loose films and jackets, and filed these in her reading room. Then, in what she referred to as her arts-and-crafts period, she took all the dictated X ray reports that Kate had signed, and glued them to their proper jackets. Once a week she went through the reading room files and purged all the discharged patients' X rays. Those X rays went back to the main X ray file room.

For this she was paid very well. The job was so simple any ten-year-old could do it. Absurd, she thought. But she only worked a thirty-two-hour week, with Wednesday and Friday afternoons off. That gave her time to drive to Berkeley for any serious research she might need for her manuscript.

To be sure, clerking was psychologically numbing. The repetitive tedium of any clerking position — and she had held many such positions in many departments in her thirteen years at the hospital — required a mindlessness most clerks found demeaning and often infuriating. Walking into the X ray file room Angie most often met eyes dilated with whatever recreational drug happened to be currently in vogue. She did not wonder that the clerks took drugs; she was outraged that administrators ignored the obvious, because to acknowledge it meant they would need to spend money humanizing a work environment.

Doctors, nurses, and aides, grown exasperated by human sickness, vented their pettiness on the clerks. The clerks responded by moving slowly, playing stupid and blind, and perversely shuffling doctors, nurses, and patients around from one person to another. "That's not my job. Why don't you call back at eight tomorrow morning?" Or "Oh, I know, but the CRT is down, the doctors are done reading for the afternoon, and that's tied up on a computer tape over in medical transcription. Call back in three days." Who dared to argue with a downed computer? "Well, yes, you rightly want a rapid reading on that patient. I understand he's on the surgery table. But Dr. Gans is on for special procedures and he's in the middle of a B.E. right now. Dr. Spearrow is out to lunch. But just as soon as the STAT person locates those films, we'll take them right up to Dr. Ashbourne. Unless, of course, you'd like to speak with my supervisor."

Any clerk was capable of dispensing with all the red tape, and doing any number of miraculous services for the right person. When treated as intelligent and responsible people, they tended to respond in a way that illuminated precisely trained minds. But few people accorded them full human status, and, treated like children, they responded in kind. All hoped to win a lottery. All hoped that competency ruled in other spheres of life because it surely didn't in the hospital.

When I was twenty-five, Angie thought, I believed in the life and death of a hospital and the service we provide. What we can do, should do. But no more. Doctors save lives, if God allows, and the rest of us save our asses.

Angie sighed quickly. Why does so much of life come down to saving your ass? History writes on such a grander scale.

But teaching, which she had done for a year, was worse. At least with this job she could leave it at the end of the day. She had time to write. The bills got paid. It was OK as long as you didn't think about it. Of course, Kate treated her as an equal. That made everything bearable.

Angie stood in line with two large cups of coffee. She surveyed the donuts respectfully. No, she thought, she wasn't hungry and sugar was out for the week. Well, maybe not the entire week. Oh, hell. She reached for a bear claw.

"Hey, Lena!" A friendly arm wrapped itself around her shoulder.

"Terry!" Angie replaced the bear claw and set the coffee on the counter. She turned and hugged Terry Palermo, a pediatric nurse working with terminally ill children. "You look great. That a new blouse? Nice color on you." Angie picked up her coffee and, because Terry was always on a diet, left the bear claw behind.

"Yeah, thanks." Terry glowed happily. "Peg gave it to me yesterday. A make up present, you know." Terry nudged Angie.

"Fighting again, huh?"

Angie often wondered how these two had stayed together for eight years. It had never been simple. She and Terry had briefly considered an affair several years ago. Circumstances had ruled that out, and they had settled for a friendship which included Thursday night bar-hopping, an occasion to vent Italian angst. "Not like the Russians, you know," Terry once observed. "They get drunk and worry about their souls. We have a few drinks and get *tormento* over love."

"The kid," Terry said with a nod. She was referring to Peg's six-year-old son.

"I've been thinking about getting a dog," Angie noted, not wanting to get into Terry's family squabble at the moment.

"Yeah, they're a lot alike, dogs and kids." Terry was looking at Angie as if she were crazy. "Maybe we could trade off on the weekends." Then another thought struck her. "Have you seen the new nurse up on C station?"

"Oh, honey," Angie moaned while her eyes did a boogie. "Personnel has been doing a little interior decorating."

"Terry." A whitely starched nurse approached them at the cash register. "How's Jimmy Nichols? Dr. Lansford admitted him last night . . ."

Coming out of the stairwell, Angie walked through the administrative office area and past admitting where she stopped and picked up the patient discharge sheet. Out in the lobby, disheveled people slumped in their chairs and stared at their feet, each person wrapped in his or her own private fear that gave way to embarrassed expectancy whenever a white-frocked doctor entered the waiting area. Her white lab coat flapping, Angie squared her shoulders and pasted a smile on her face as she walked by.

Taking a right turn, she passed the elevators and pushed open the door into the doctors' reading area. Six office doors led off the small lobby.

Angie considered the number of doors in a hospital. People, already in a state of confusion due to their own illness or the illness of a friend, could never possibly grasp the intricate logic of all these doors. The hospital was a secret world. It took as much luck as determination to find the proper door in or out. If one viewed oneself in either category — in or out — the battle was lost. Most people sat where they were told — waiting — and never ventured into the grim corridors with their forbidding doors. But a patient truly could prowl at will through this labyrinth; the staff cared little for confrontation, and became annoyed only when asked for directions. The annoyance wasn't so much with the patients as with the unlikelihood of giving adequate directions. Six doors and ten turns might advance a person only twelve feet. The effect was paralytic. The fear in some patients' eyes equalled the vacancy in those who couldn't stay with the fear and simply turned their minds off. Well, if the weaknesses of people became magnified in the hospital so too did the courage and goodness.

She returned to the hospital reading room.

"The urinary bladder appears slightly deviated to the right..."

Angie worked to the rhythmic technical drone of Kate's dictating voice which was hypnotically comforting, as much company as a radio. Taking the lid off her coffee, she looked through the three pages of discharges. Appleton had left — celebration had erupted on G station ten seconds after he'd exited. Baby Boy Wendel, a preemie with two jackets of chest films, had gone home. The staff in the nursery had fallen in love with him, and the separation had been painful even though devoutly wished. Angie sipped her coffee.

At eleven forty-five, Alex, as trim as an exclamation mark, danced into the reading room. Although the certificate in his office attested to his right to practice podiatry, his pink cheeks and exuberant aura reflected his real love — sports medicine.

At the sight of him, Angie sprang from her chair and into his arms. "Alex, let's dance." She looked into brown eyes that held her as lightly as his arms which gently swirled her in elegant circles.

"How's my favorite clerk?" he asked as he dipped her backwards. "Ready for lunch?"

"Now I'm jealous," Kate cut in. "You can dance together, but when Alex starts talking food to other women ..."

They all laughed as Alex reached for Kate's hand and with tender courtlinesss pulled her from her chair, kissing the corner of her mouth as she rose.

Chapter 3

On Tuesday afternoon Kate and Angie walked through the glass doors of the Universal Fitness Health Spa. Angie, who had protested the location of this spa as being in the wrong part of town, wrinkled her nose in complaint. The fetid thickness of human perspiration trickled up from the utilitarian carpet like shimmering waves of heat off the 120 degree summer pavement on the industrial street outside.

A skeletal thread of a woman, in two-inch black heels and wearing a black leotard under a baby blue smock, approached them in a flutter of inefficient energy. She did not look healthy, Angie critically observed; black lines under her hollow eyes accentuated a sallow complexion. Angie had grown accustomed to her own health, and Kate's rosy tan served as a mirror in which Angie saw her own wholesomeness reflected. With the innate prejudice of the seasoned lesbian she suspected makeup as an attempt to either conceal beauty or hide imperfection. Rarely did women use makeup to enhance nature. Kate's full lips had a natural deep plum stain that with the simple application of colorless lip moisturizer gave the impression of finished cosmetics without, however, the involvement of artificial colors. The blue eye shadow and pasty complexion descending on them now was a disadvertisement for the whole health industry.

"Hello." With a friendly smile Kate greeted the woman. "We have an appointment to be put on a weight training program."

"Yeah, hi. I'm Shelly. First ya have to sign in, right? Over here on this sheet. Every time ya come in. Then ya want to put your bags and stuff in a locker. Come on, I'll show ya the lockers . . ."

Kate hurriedly signed the sheet, and she and Shelly headed for the back area while Angie, miffed over a sign-in sheet — Big Brother was everywhere — wrote down a false name and followed a truculent twelve feet behind.

Reflected by floor to ceiling mirrors, perhaps ten women were working out in the front part of the gym, sweating over stationary bikes or lifting dumbbells, their vacant stares set in a retarded-like concentration. In the back half of the gym an aerobic dance class was in progress. Angie carefully picked her way around flailing arms and kicking feet which worked in varying degrees of approximation to the rhythm of *Fame.* With military

31

precision the instructor yelled out to her charges —
"Lift-two-three!" — while pudgy wrinkled white-haired
women vied with full-bodied middle-aged ladies and
multi-layered punk youth to duplicate the intricate
movements demonstrated. Angie smiled ruefully and
kicked her foot to the music: Kate *had* to be out of her
mind!

Accompanied by Shelly, Kate and Angie placed their
belongings in a locker. If they had valuables they must
bring their own locks — the spa could not be responsible
for lost goods, Shelly explained. She pointed to the sauna
and whirlpool. Kate smiled pleasantly. Angie frowned.
They returned to the front reception area with its bulletin
board displaying the woman of the month — her name
was Karen and she had lost forty-five pounds. Various
lists of statistics competed for attention together with the
inspirational motto for June — "A friend is someone who
encourages you to look your best." Angie studied a
pulse-rate chart.

Kate weighed in at 142, perfect for her 5′8″ frame.
Measurements: 35″ chest, 26″ waist, 36″ hips, 22″ thigh —
Shelly, void of emotional response, noted it all on Kate's
new chart as she announced the numbers out loud. And
how much weight did Kate want to lose?

"What!" Angie jumped in. "You think this woman
needs to lose weight? Just look at this body. Kate runs
marathons for chrissake! She needs to build a little
muscle in her upper body maybe. That's all." Indignant,
Angie looked at Shelly as she would a misbehaving child.

"Angelina, please." Kate turned her eyes on her
friend, both embarrassed and flattered by Angie's
outburst. "Maybe I *would* like to lose a little weight."

Shelly looked up and smiled gratefully at Kate. The eyes almost came to life. She moved down to measure Kate's calf.

"Kate is not your average sedentary person," Angie informed Shelly. She knew she should shut up, and she would in a minute, but she wanted the last word. "Doesn't sit in front of the TV eating bonbons all day, you know."

"Most of the women here don't do that either, ma'am," Shelly stated flatly. "They spend long days cleanin house and fixin dinner. Sometimes they get so twisted round they eat as much as they put on the table. Now they're tryin to do somethin for theirselves. They're tryin for sure."

Angie, embarrassed, blushed. There was more wisdom in this woman's twang than there was compassion in her own quick tongue. *Damn my opinionated mouth!* Kate looked at her and winked. Angie shook her head and looked at the floor. At least Kate still loved her.

"Julie," Shelly called to an idle worker. "Will ya com'ere a minute. This is Kate and Angie. I wanta test Kate on the bike. Would ya mind takin Angie's measurements? I started the chart. Here." Shelly handed the chart to Julie, and with a smile to her, walked off. Kate waved a few fingers at Angie and followed.

One hundred-eighteen pounds! Angie held her breath and slammed her eyes shut. This would never do! Marie Antoinette might eat cake but then with a mother like Maria Theresa for a model and no bathroom scales, what did she know?

"What's the waist measurement?" Angie braced for the guillotine blade. The two pounds she'd gained were probably in the waist, she told herself.

"Twenty-three," Julie answered as she moved to the hips.

Oh, Christ, Angie moaned to herself. First the fall of Rome and now the fall of my stomach. Gravity. Whatever happened to my twenty-two inch waist? Six miles tomorrow. No question about it. Should up my pace too. Twenty-three inches!

After their workout Angie and Kate sat nude in the sauna. Angie appraised Kate's body appreciatively. What, she wondered, was a lesbian even doing in a place such as this? She'd have to talk it over with Terry.

Kate broke into her thoughts: "What do you think?"

"No doubt about it. You've got a beautiful body." Angie smiled and looked at the wood-planked floor.

"Not that, sweetie." Kate smiled. She could always count on Angie to speak the first thing on her mind. "What do you think of the gym?"

"The workout was nothing. I get more exercise tossing X ray jackets around." Warming to her subject, Angie continued, "Besides, they put you on that exercise bike to test your cardiovascular fitness, and then tell you you're not up to potential. Your working pulse rate should be higher? I don't buy it. Katie, your resting pulse rate is what? Fifty? It's already very low because you're a long distance runner — naturally it's not going to zoom up there like some person who can't walk around the block without getting winded. I just don't think this place is geared for a serious athlete like you." Angie, who had read extensively about physical fitness since Kate had asked for her support, now felt like an expert on the subject.

"Wait till tomorrow," Kate said. "You'll discover aching muscles in places you didn't know you had muscles. Trust me." At least Kate hoped so. Angie could be right, she reflected. That bike business didn't seem right to her either. "It takes time, Angie. You don't get instant gratification on this one."

"I've just been insulted!" Angie turned indignantly on Kate. "Are you suggesting I only go for instant gratification? What kind of person do you think I am? Is this what you think of me?"

"Now, sweetie, you know if I said let's forget the whole thing you'd be the first to drop your barbell and flee this establishment."

Angie laughed, sweat dripping from her face. Kate smiled back, thinking that if Paul Klee did animal portraits Angie would now appear as a drenched skunk — her thick black hair matted around slightly protruding ears, and her large eyes looking bigger because she insisted on wearing sunglasses when she ran and therefore the white surrounding her eyes stood out against the darkness of her face.

"So why are we sitting here offering up our body fluids, Katie?"

"What do you mean?"

"Well, really. Don't we sweat enough when we run? Five minutes here isn't going to purify our bodies any more than a thirty minute run, right?" What would Kate do without me, Angie wondered. Sometimes she just didn't cover all the angles.

"I'll talk with Alex about it. I suspect you're right." Kate hated to admit this, hated to admit that she might be wasting Angie's time. Suddenly she became irritated with

Angie. The woman's questioning mind could drive a sane person crazy. Didn't she ever rest?

"While you're working on the facts, doctor, this body is working on dehydration."

"Oh, come on. Doesn't it feel good?"

"You're serious?" Perhaps Kate was *really* serious. "My nose burns every time I take a deep breath which —" Angie held up an arm, "I'd rather not do because it stinks in here. My earrings are repiercing my ears — metal's a marvelous conductor, isn't it? And I don't like to sweat. Elemental. God knows how many ladies have dampened the wood whereon I sit. Sitting in someone else's sweat is pretty intimate, don't you think? Oh, Katie, could I tell my mother about this?"

"You couldn't tell your mother about half your life. It's x-rated." Kate turned on her friend and took her neck between two damp hands, shaking her playfully. Your mother'd die if she knew you were sleeping with a woman twice your age!"

"Rochelle is not seventy-six!" Angie giggled back at Kate. "Besides, I thought you'd be understanding about such things. Alex is half your age."

"Let's do something else," Kate ordered, annoyed with Angie's comment.

"You don't have to ask me twice." Angie grabbed her towel and followed Kate.

"Oh, Christ!" Angie sat up to her neck in whirling water. "Someone's going to serve us boiled for dinner tonight. Minestrone soup. This water has got to be two hundred degrees."

"Angie, sweetie, look at me and read my lips. I'm tired of listening to you bitch. One more complaint and you go sit in the car."

What had she been thinking of when she asked Angie to work out with her? Come to think of it, Angie was not someone you'd want to share a foxhole with — she'd complain that bullets were being fired. No, that wasn't fair, Kate admitted. You'd just have to explain everything to her first — about war and bullets and foxholes.

Angie studied Kate. Maybe she had gone too far. *Celebration* came over the sound system. Angie bounced her shoulders to the music.

"Want to go out dancing tonight, Kate?" She gave Kate a playful smile by way of apologizing for all the bitching. "We spend too much time working together. We should play more. Meet me in the sandlot behind the school track?" Angie's dimples creased up to her high cheekbones.

Kate laughed. "Not tonight, sweetie. We could go out to eat, however."

"Ah ha! Going for the gusto again," Angie teased, and leaned her head back onto the tiles. "You must have been an Italian mama in your past life."

They sat in the whirlpool, occasionally changing positions so that the water jets hit all the proper places. Like a Buddha, Kate closed her eyes in meditation. She patted the blonde braid she wore wrapped up on the top of her head and which had wilted in the moist heat. Looking at Angie through eyeslits, seeing a maturity in Angie's tired eyes that belied the glibness of her tongue, Kate felt a tenderness that bordered on the sexual. Shared fatigue, she told herself. But what if it were a man sitting across from her . . . What were the boundaries? And why did it matter so much if one crossed over them?

She had never thought too much about Angie's homosexuality. She had known Angie as a friend before she had learned of her lesbianism. The two of them shared similar values; the same kind of humor bound them together. Angie didn't spend all her time talking about the men she dated or medicine or floor polish. Nothing wrong with those subjects, Kate admitted, but they wore thin with the years. Nor had Angie ever flaunted her sexuality. In fact, it had been one of the doctors who'd told her. He had tried repeatedly to date Angie, and Kate at first considered his accusation sour grapes. But when she laughingly mentioned it to Angie, Angie had shrugged in a what-can-you-do-about-it attitude, and said that well actually she *was* a little bit lesbian. Kate discovered that she was not greatly surprised. It was like discovering that your grandmother had had an affair. Besides, Kate considered, who was she to pass judgment on an issue that had never really struck her one way or another?

Alex's only comment had been "What a waste," to which she defensively replied, "I doubt that the women in her life feel that way." Funny how men looked at these things.

"Did you hear the conversation on the floor?" Angie cut into Kate's thoughts.

"No." Kate was sorry for the interruption.

"This one woman was talking about how her husband nearly shot her this morning . . ."

"Every family has its ups and downs."

"Bad line, Eleanor of Hepburn. It was the rapist."

"Her husband?" Kate asked indifferently, her eyes closed again.

"No. She got up at four this morning and was taking a shower. Thought she heard something. Look, everyone but you is on edge about this rapist. So she screamed. Her husband jumps out of bed, still half asleep, and lunges for the shotgun in the closet and he falls as his wife comes running into the bedroom. Out of the closet he comes dripping clothes and brandishing his gun. He suddenly recognizes his wife and instead of shooting her, pumps the shot into the water bed. Woke up half the neighborhood. Water all over the place." As Angie related the story she acted out the events so that waves splashed over the tiles in the whirlpool.

"Angie! What if he'd shot her?" Kate was appalled. "Guns should be outlawed. And you've gone out and bought one." She shook her head. "This rapist absolutely controls the city. A man nearly kills his wife trying to protect her. If irony were a good substitute for tragedy, I'd laugh. This is insanity."

"You should've heard the women out there, Kate. Peace-loving women talking about cutting the rapist's balls off. They're serious. Reminds me of a line from Strindberg I was rereading last week: 'Life is so strange. So against me, so vindictive that I became vindictive too . . .' The women are really scared, Kate."

"How does Strindberg figure into the Black Crow?" Kate was relieved at what looked like a change of subject. The Black Crow was a turn-of-the-century tavern, in Berlin, into which any number of important cultural figures had wandered. *The Black Crow* was also the working title of Angie's manuscript. "He was a misogynist playwright."

"Probably more tortured than anything else. He wrote *Swanwhite* for his third wife — the play was brimful of magic and romance. Of course," Angie shrugged, "by the time he finished the play they were divorced. I think he had the temperament of an artist but was cursed with the social conditioning, the morals, of a Puritan. Not a great mix. The artist in him fell in love with these free-spirited women he was attracted to, but the moralist in him was appalled. Then too, physical love for him always seemed to bring hatred in its wake. But he and his third wife remained friends. That was progress for Strindberg." Angie paused and looked at Kate.

Kate smiled encouragement, and waited for the story to continue.

"However, that was not what we were talking about, Katie. Doesn't anything frighten you? The rapist doesn't seem to. Do you sleep well at night?" Angie peered at Kate playfully. "You can tell me, we're friends."

"Sometimes I don't sleep so well at night," Kate conceded reluctantly; she felt herself shift inside, and held her breath against a potential avalanche of emotions. Steady girl, she told herself. Angie isn't looking for anything deep.

But she went on, "I guess compared to what frightens others, my fears aren't too many or too great. Last night I dreamed I was in the hospital having open heart surgery. In the midst of the operation, with all those tubes coming out of my body, I had to go down to the parking lot to see my mother. She had brought me a plate of peas. I hate peas! She knows that. Of course, dutiful daughter that I am, I don't tell her about my operation and she doesn't notice the opened red cavity of my chest or the tubes hanging . . ." Kate drifted off, suddenly re-experiencing the unease she had felt last night upon waking. She hadn't been able to get back to sleep, and had read until it was time to get up.

"Then what happened?" Angie asked with concern, all thoughts of Strindberg forgotten.

Kate shook her head. "I ate the peas. What else?" She sighed, and laughed softly, trying to cover her embarrassment.

It took all of Angie's good sense and training as a rape crisis counselor to remain silent. She reached across the water and stroked Kate's cheek lightly. What, she wondered, was the pain so greatly feared that only a dream could hit at it?

Kate looked at Angie as if awakening from the dream she had just described. She smiled a tired smile. "Let's get out of here. It *is* hot." She stood up, water flowing down her body.

Angie stood up with her, reached for her arm, and leaning into Kate's body whispered into her ear — "My life is richer because of you."

Chapter 4

The Boeing 747 fell off the embankment into fifty feet of ocean, and it was only because August Strindberg had blown out a window with his submachine gun that Kate and Angie, sitting at the instrument panel, escaped. A tubercular child, an oval mouth for a face, fell out of an Edvard Munch painting. Angie felt herself swimming out of the child's mouth, searching for Kate and the ocean's surface. Her childhood became mixed with images from her manuscript; she was four years old, wrapped in a white sheet. She became the skeletal child of Munch's painting, eaten by tuberculosis and maggots, clawing out of a grave and choking on Mendocino dirt.

Angie sat bolt upright, gasping for air, arms urgently flailing in an attempt to peel away layered darkness. She jumped out of bed, grabbed her head between both hands, and doubled over in an agony of terror. She slammed the palm of her hand against a wall. "Motherfucker! That son of a bitch!"

Rochelle slept on, serene in her own dreams. Angie hurled herself at the bed, and like water scattered into a hot skillet, ricocheted around the sleeping form. "Wake up! *Vita brevos! Basta!* At least Nero fiddled while Rome burned. You . . . you'd sleep!" Furiously Angie shook Rochelle.

"What?" Rochelle half-opened her eyes. The excitement in Angie's voice roused her only slightly. "What's the matter, hon?"

Too late Angie realized that her display of excitement no longer roused Rochelle. While her husband might be a study in contrast, Rochelle didn't see him that often — he was always out of town on business. Hell, she didn't even see her children that often, Angie fumed. Rochelle spent her days in art museums — they had met in one — or shopping in San Francisco. A live-in maid took care of the children.

"Never mind." Angie removed her hands from Rochelle's shoulders and jumped out of bed. What was she doing with this woman anyway? She was no comfort, no companion. *She warms my bed and tickles my fancy. When the mood hits her. Grow up, Lena, you dumb ass!*

Angie stomped into the kitchen, flung open a drawer, grabbed her address book, picked up the telephone, looked for her brother's number, and dialed.

43

"Nunzio, you limp prick!" Her anger leaped like a starving rat across the miles to Los Angeles. "You scum! You buried me alive! Four years old. I trusted you, you *castrato*. You fettucini brain. I adored you, you . . ."

Angie hung up, and shook. Tears tumbled off her chin and splashed onto the kitchen counter. How could he have done that to her? Her brother, the monsignor. Mother's pride. Her buddy who took her fishing and kissed her knees when she scraped them. How?

Sirens stabbed the four o'clock silence outside. Angie thought of the rapist, and realized that she felt no fear, only a thumping hurt localized in her chest, her throat. All those years ago her brother had held her down, tied her hands, gagged her, and wrapped her in a small sheet. She thought it was a game. Then he buried her alive! No wonder she feared being tied down; the thought of someone lying on her made her frantic. She had never understood. It was her brother. How could he? How could he?

The phone rang. She picked it up on the first ring, but said nothing.

"Lena, *bambino*. I'm sorry. That was a *scherzo* — we didn't know. We were just little boys — not evil, just *capriccioso* egging each other on . . ." There was a tired urgency in his pastoral voice, a compassion filled with intensity that Angie always associated with him. No wonder she had blocked out the burial. Nunzio never did anything wrong.

"A joke?" Angie whispered into the phone. "Nunzio, Nunzio. You were my older brother. You were the center of my life. Mama and Papa had all the other kids to take care of. It was you who took care of me . . ."

"Forgive me, Lena. I can't justify what I did. I guess because you never said anything I took that to mean it hadn't really upset you. Well, that's not true either," he hedged. Angie said nothing. "I wanted it not to matter. It couldn't have been more than three or four minutes. Somehow you must have had a pocket of air in there. I dug you out with my hands . . . and cried. You didn't talk to anyone for two days. Papa wanted to take you to the doctor's. Said some *accidenti* befell you. I was scared and followed you around. But then you snapped out of it, started talking like nothing had happened. We were friends again and if anything I felt more protective than before. I vowed nothing bad would ever happen to you . . ."

"Is that why you call me two or three times a month, to ease your conscience?"

"Oh, Lena, no. You are the only woman in my life." There was agony in his voice. "I'm so sorry that happened. Is there anything I can say? What brought this up now?"

"A dream," she said quickly. "Maybe the stress of the book I'm working on and . . . this rapist has been terrorizing Sacramento. I have an unreasonable fear of being tied down. I never understood why. Why did you do it, Nunzio? *Non capisco.*"

"Sweetheart, I'm embarrassed to tell you. I have gone to confession over this more than once — I know that doesn't help you," he added softly. "But it was *the* sin of my childhood, and maybe all my sins tied up in one example. Pride, ambition. I know, I know, that's not your concern. We — we were reenacting the Corpus Christi. I got to play, you know, the priest. It was my idea. Naturally. I had white sheets for vestments. I had some matches, and lit some dry hay for incense. It was my love of show, of display. Maybe ritual. We needed a corpus. Lena, you were the smallest one. You were the perfect baby Jesus. You just looked at me with those trusting eyes . . . Oh, I felt so powerful . . ."

Angie could feel the apology in his voice, the sadness. She knew from years of talking with him that he truly considered pride to be his greatest weakness — that he flogged himself mentally for this sin. She also considered him the tenderest man she knew, that his calling was a perfect match of aptitude with position. This man would have never made it in the normal storm and stress of intimate relations; God was his buffer. He served his God well, and because he did, Angie felt relieved of that family responsibility. He counseled her. He prayed for her. He never condemned. He accepted her. He, as much as Kate or Terry, was her friend. He was family.

"Lena, is there anything I can do?" He cut into her silence. "Are you there?"

"Ah, Nunzio . . ." Angie's voice was tired. "How am I going to get into heaven on your skirt tails if you do stuff like this?"

"Can I come up and spend some time with you?"

"Not right now. I need some time for myself. Could you come up in late September? We could go backpacking."

"I would like that. I'll clear my calendar."

A glass of warm milk in her stomach, Angie moved her body into Rochelle's and placed her arms around the comatose form. Maybe Strindberg and Munch and that whole company of demented men who met at the Black Crow would now leave her alone. Strindberg hadn't wanted to kill her; he had meant only to get her attention and wake her up. The man was psychic even in death. Munch's "Scream" had helped her voice her own scream.

46

The comforts of art; a bridge to mysterious realities. She smiled grimly, but at the same time felt at peace.

She stroked Rochelle's gray head. The sweetness of her perfume, Raffinee, mixed with the natural sweetness of her flesh, flooded Angie's senses. She ran her tongue over Rochelle's shoulder.

Rochelle stirred, turned over into the embrace of her lover, and kissed her neck.

"Everything OK?" she asked, sleep slipping off her words like drops of ice cream on a warm day. "Come closer. You're cold, sweetheart."

Angie placed her half-open mouth on Rochelle's, and wondered if it would ever be possible to get any closer. She had grown accustomed to the physical comfort of Rochelle — long nights of loving. But she had to honestly admit that the days were empty, the conversation never satisfying unless it ended in orgasm. How did Rochelle really feel about anything? Or — the thought was only beginning to form — did Rochelle feel anything at all?

"Tell me how you felt at five, Rochelle." Angie nibbled at her ear.

"Boring question, Lena." With somnolent indifference Rochelle turned over.

Angie felt the verbal rejection more intensely than the physical. Rochelle had turned away emotionally once too often. Suddenly Angie knew she had been living with the expectation that somehow Rochelle would open up to her. But in the year they had been seeing each other that had never happened. Rochelle was the product of imagination. She brought pleasure in thought and anticipation, she was a beautiful picture. But her actual presence brought only fleeting satisfaction. Angie knew that she had given her love to a dream image.

47

Tears came to Angie's eyes. She turned away, and as she did so, pain seeping from her heart, she took her love, homeless and grieving, away with her.

* * * * *

Shelly Machenzie drove into her driveway. It was a warm summer night, perhaps eighty degrees. Hank Williams blared from the car radio, through her open car window, across the treeless front yard of the new tract house. The health club, empty of patrons, had closed at 11:00, a whole hour early, and Shelly, exhausted, felt grateful for the extra time.

She rested her head on the steering wheel and listened to the song. One more night in the empty house. Her husband, Drew, would be in the hospital at least another two months. He was a truck mechanic, and two months ago a driver, mistaking Drew's instructions, had started one of the rigs while Drew was still under it. The semi-rig had dropped on his back. Now he was paralyzed from the neck down. Shelly knew he would rather be dead. She was thankful he was alive, and she felt guilty knowing she would selfishly keep him alive, even breathe for him, just to hear his voice. Too tired to put the car in the garage, too indifferent to roll up the windows, she turned off the radio and got out of the car. The phrase dog-tired slid numbly through her mind.

Sissy, their German Shepherd, ran happily toward her as she entered the house. "Hi, girl," Shelly greeted the dog who proceeded to run circles around her, knocking into her thin legs, slurping at her hands with a wet tongue. "Bet ya wanta pee, huh?" Shelly bent over and hugged the large dog. "Come on. Out back wit ya."

She undressed down to her underpants, and looked at the bed. She had to be up at six tomorrow, same as every morning now that Drew was in the hospital. Should she shower? No, it was too hot and she'd only sweat in bed, necessitating another shower in the morning. Since Drew

49

was in the hospital — the event by which she now measured everything — she had been conserving on the energy bill. No need to smell good in bed now anyway, she thought.

She walked back into the bathroom for a drink of water. Sissy barked. She barked again, and Shelly was on the verge of going to the back porch when she heard a tapping at the bedroom window. The tapping grew louder as she ran back into the bedroom. Sissy had stopped barking. Shelly started down the hall, then abruptly turned and walked back into the bedroom. She took the thirty-eight from the night stand and checked to see if it was loaded. Her knees weakened momentarily as she remembered the last winter day when Drew had taken her out target shooting. Longing and fear filled her stomach in equal measure.

Why had Sissy stopped barking? Physically calm, she walked back down the hall, looked out the dining room window. The night was black. Sissy was nowhere in sight. Shelly checked the gun one more time as she picked up the phone and dialed the police emergency number.

Put on hold, she cocked the gun. She heard glass break in the bedroom. Her heart flipped back and forth like a fish tossed on land. A woman came to the phone.

"I'm Shelly Machenzie . . . I don't have time to tell ya the spellin, lady. Someone just busted in my bedroom window. I live at 46221 Lilac Lane . . . Lady, someone's comin down the hall right now. You get someone out here! Zip is 95628. Ya get someone out here now!"

What had happened to Sissy? If anything's happened to Sissy . . . Anger pounded at her temples. With the gun held out in front of her, her eyes on the hallway, Shelly edged slowly through the living room toward the front door. A large shadow filled the hall wall. She saw a gloved

50

hand on the door frame, and fired the gun with both hands, nearly jerked off the floor as she did so.

"I gotta gun here, mister! Ya move and I'll blow your shit away!" Backing into the front door, Shelly opened it slowly with one hand. Like a suddenly broken dam, she turned and plunged out the front door, spilling across the front yard and out into the street.

Had she not been early he would have been in her bedroom when she got home. In her house! Drew had been going to put in an alarm system. And a garage door opener. And a sodium floodlight in the backyard. Oh, God! No more, no more! She sat down on the warm street pavement, her jaw clenched, and with the gun held straight out in front of her, waited for the police.

Five minutes later a patrol car, cruising slowly down Lilac Lane, came to a quiet halt before a skinny, nearly naked young woman. Except for the visible shaking of arms, the form was rigidly frozen in concentration, gun pointing toward a front door.

"Must be the place, Joe."

"Yep," Joe answered grimly.

Chapter 5

In bed, Kate pointed her toes and stretched her calves. The muscles in her legs responded more promptly than her mind which, clinging to the disoriented clutter of a dream, pulled her back into floating shadows. The parking lot of a suburban shopping mall, some catastrophe, already plasticized cadavers with a few expressionless doctors performing autopsies . . . Appalled but curious, she did not force herself awake. Where was she in the dream? Remote, observing, always the student, she stood on the sidelines researching national emergencies with a medical book. Without opening her eyes, she rolled over in the king-size bed, drew her knees up to her chest, and placed her cheek on Alex's warm arm.

I'm not even a pathologist! Painfully she thought back to the first month of her internship. Her first rotation had been on the gynecology ward at Davis Medical Center. It was not a typical ward; almost all of the patients had advanced cancer. With most of their insides removed, these women had bags in which to urinate and tubes through which food was pumped into their bodies.

Welcome to the world of medicine, she reflected. We were trained to save lives, so we thumped silent hearts and pushed air into dead lungs. Someday she would be trained to bring a patient back to life who was not already irretrievably lost to cancer. But she couldn't hold out for someday.

With shame she reminded herself that it had finally been the odor of unembalmed flesh — bodies festered to ripeness and fermentation through medical obstinance — that drove her away from patient treatment. The stink of the ward had filled even her sleeping hours, and for a month she vomited, not able to keep any food down. She had lost over twenty pounds. Relief outweighed shame when she finally discovered the odorless world of radiology. Yet the memory always hurt. She seldom thought of herself as a real doctor. Though others accorded her that title, she thought of herself as a well-paid technician. Second best. A woman who couldn't deal with hard realities.

She raised her head enough to see over Alex's chest, a chest covered with soft curly auburn hair. The red digits of the clock registered 6:10. She could hear rain gently breaking on the roof. She couldn't remember rain in June, but the forecast called for two days of it. Kate smiled to herself. Although Sacramento summer nights cooled down to fifty degrees, by ten in the morning it could be eighty outside, too hot to run. With this morning's rain she could loiter with the missing sun, run later. She placed her cheek back on Alex's arm, and roamed contentedly in his musty scent.

Getting out of bed, she walked into the kitchen. She couldn't eat anything solid and still run, so breakfast consisted of a protein drink — yogurt, orange juice, milk, and a variety of powdered vitamins and amino acids. Kate threw all this into the blender, rupturing the kitchen's silence with its screeching whir. She removed some French roast coffee beans from the freezer, ground them in an electric grinder, and poured boiling water through the drip filter into the coffee pot. Silly to wash all these vitamins down with caffeine, she scolded herself even while joyfully inhaling the aroma now prowling the room. But caffeine was an addiction and the vitamins would simply have to work around it. Vitamins, she firmly believed, were the secret to her health. Well, she was healthy and she took vitamins; the two *could* be related. She turned off the blender and poured her drink.

Glass in hand, Kate gazed out the kitchen window into the backyard. Refracted droplets of moisture sparkled off the lawn even while the light drizzle cast the day in a confetti of grays. The protein drink, made with strawberry yogurt, slid down her throat as smoothly as a milkshake.

Why all the morbid thoughts lately, she wondered. Am I losing my mind, my grip? No, I just need a good run. Ashbourne's remedy for a woman in crisis — a twenty-mile run. She smiled ruefully. What crisis? Cadavers in your dreams and oncology wards before breakfast don't constitute a crisis. Just an occupational hazard. Godammit! I've done better than most women my age! So my marriage to Gary didn't make it through medical school. Lots of relationships don't survive the time demands of med school. I'm no different than anyone else, she reassured herself. I don't have to prove anything. There isn't any crisis. I'm just concentrating on my failures this morning. No, these are *not* failures! The Olympics — that's a failure. No children . . .

Maybe Dan had been a failure. She thought back to the financial consultant she had lived with for three years after her marriage — until he had insisted on marriage and children. At first she had interpreted his demand as a pitch for respectability, that social approval mattered more than living with her. But she came to appreciate what Dan wanted and stood for. Dan was a mentally healthy man who approached life like a team sport. In the world of high finance the right kind of wife was an asset, to be sure. Yet she also understood that he wanted to share the game with her, wanted a partner. He did not think of people as assets. She hadn't married him, and she had loved him. She hadn't been in love with him — maybe *that* was her failure. As nearly as she could tell, she simply didn't fall in love like other women.

And Daddy, she thought, disgust rising like acid in her stomach. Why had she been thinking of him again? Three years of therapy — surely she was over all that. She now saw clearly how incest had colored her other relationships, making intimacy impossible. It had taken years of effort, but she had learned how to stay present in sexual relationships — how not to dissociate from the present. Alex was not her father and she was not twelve. She was not repeating a cycle of molestation. She was learning to trust people, to be more open. She was fine. Healthy and in control.

The garage door leading into the family room swung open with a bang and Scott loped in, his slick black racing shorts topping long thin muscular legs. His six-foot frame came to an abrupt halt when he noticed Kate's startled look across the open counter space from the kitchen.

"Morning, sister!" He filled the room with easy cheer.

"Up awfully early for a rainy day, Scotty," Kate commented with a smile.

"My type A personality. Forty miles this morning. The bike's running good."

"My God! What time did you get up?" Although Kate could run twenty miles, the distances Scott rode staggered her.

"Four. How 'bout some coffee?" Scott moved into the kitchen and reached for a towel to dry his face and short-cropped light brown hair.

"Let me get it." Kate affectionately brushed his arm with her hand as she walked past him to the stove.

She was proud of Scott's accomplishments in biking. Only three years older than he, she wondered how much of his adulthood was in reaction to her childhood. She had worked for straight A's and gone to medical school while Scott had squeezed through high school and gone into construction work. She had had few friends — spent her after-school time with the track team, and seldom brought anyone home. Scott, always in trouble, brought every delinquent in Sacramento into the family house. Always mother's pet, he sullenly endured his father's criticism, given only when Mother wasn't around to protect him. Then he stopped coming home, staying away for days at a time. He hadn't straightened out until their parents moved to Florida and he took up biking.

With their parents gone, Kate and Scott had moved back into the family house. The large family room with its own bathroom and upstairs bedroom was Scott's half of the house. The living room and three back bedrooms belonged to Kate. The kitchen was communal.

Because of their respect for each other, the arrangement had worked out well. Scott might bring friends home from work on Friday nights, but then Kate usually spent Fridays with Alex. What little entertaining Kate did she planned for when Scott was out of town at a bike race. She assumed he had women friends, but seldom saw him with any. Since Scott went to work early or planned early morning bike rides, he usually went to bed around nine. Although she was aware that Scott didn't fully approve of her sleep-in arrangement with Alex, of such things they seldom spoke. Still, he liked Alex. They got along in an easy, friendly way.

As Scott accepted the coffee he said, "Been thinking of riding in the Coors Classic next year." He laid this out more slowly than usual, well aware of Kate's politics and her boycott of Coors products.

"Really?" Kate tried to sound approving. She thought she understood Scott's right-wing politics: His number had never been drawn in the Vietnam draft and because flag waving was required in the construction industry, Scott must have over-compensated by zealously mouthing John Birch dogma. Now he believed it. If only Adlai Stevenson had been elected president, she reasoned, all this could have been avoided.

"You know I'm representing the club in the Bastille Day race in Mendocino next month?" His pride was matter-of-fact.

"Good for you!"

"Say, why don't you and Alex come up for the race? Bring Angie. It would be nice to have family around in the winner's circle. Besides, you owe me for the drive to San Francisco for that race you ran in March."

"That's true." Kate thought a moment. "It would be a fun weekend actually. Good idea." Kate felt guilty for not attending more of Scott's races. A competitor herself, she knew the importance of having someone in the crowd cheering for you. But she was pleased now because, at least according to her reading, Scott was including Alex and Angie in their small family of two. Why he was including Angie she couldn't figure — except that Angie was now staying in the cottage behind the house, and Scott spent a good deal of time talking with her. Maybe he was attracted to her. Wouldn't be the first man, Kate smiled to herself.

"It's July seventeenth. I'm staying with Aunt Jane and Uncle Jerry. A friend of mine has reservations at the National Hotel but he won't be going, so you and Alex can have his room."

"You have it all figured out, hotshot. What about Angie?"

"Angie has that ex-lover up there — Sheila, I think. The painter. They're still good friends. She was just talking the other day about going up and visiting."

"You keep track of Angie's lovers?" Kate teased.

"Only the pretty ones who want to do my portrait." Scott puffed out his chest. "She thinks I'm handsome."

"You know Sheila?" Kate only vaguely remembered her. She *could* remember Angie's pain four years ago when Sheila had moved away. It was out of that broken affair that she and Angie had become close friends, going out to dinner and to movies together. Angie took her to art shows, while she had recommended Thomas Mann to Angie for light reading. Kate had the feeling that she and Thomas Mann had helped Angie muddle through the break-up. Straight or gay, divorce is the same, Kate reflected.

"Tuned her car once." Scott smiled broadly at Kate, and his face, leathered through outdoor exposure, wrinkled kindly. "Good coffee."

As Kate poured more, Scott walked over and hugged her. "Think I'll shower and get some shuteye, sis. Ask Alex about the race."

"Scotty," Kate called softly to his retreating back, "you are not now nor have you ever been a type A personality. And I'm glad."

He turned, shrugged, and gave her a lazy smile. "Night, sis."

Kate set two cups of coffee on the nightstand and, removing her knee length T-shirt, slid under the covers. Alex stirred. Kate positioned her body next to him, placed her head on his shoulder and draped an arm over his chest. She loved the definition of his chest, the rise of his pectoral muscles. Working out only three days a week, he lacked the large muscles of a bodybuilder, but the tight youthful muscles he did possess excited her. She nibbled on his ear.

"Don't go away," he whispered. "I'll be right back, Ruth." He opened one eye as he got out of bed and shuffled out of the room.

"Ruth?" Kate yelled after him. "Ruth who?"

"Oh, my God!" Alex stuck his head around the corner and opened both eyes. "This is Sunday morning. You must be Kate. Honey, if you'd only marry me we could avoid this embarrassment." He ducked into the bathroom.

Kate smiled at his bantering. She heard him brushing his teeth. He had proposed a year and a half ago, had mentioned it periodically since in a matter-of-fact way, never nagging and only occasionally teasing. He was passively confident that she would marry him, and his confidence comforted her. She did not want to be pushed into a decision, although she did sometimes fear that he might withdraw his love or go in search of someone younger, someone who could give him children and joyfully do his laundry. In moments of perfect clarity she could see him with a beautiful young woman his own age, established in a neat suburban home, starting a family — the perfect husband and father. Part of that was a projection of her own longing for what she would never have, and part of it was an unselfish wish for the man she loved. But then in other moments of uncharacteristic anxiety she thought she had better marry him before he did leave.

After a year and a half with him, she knew that time would not answer her problem. Soon *he* would know that time would not answer the question either. Her fear now was that out of embarrassment over the lapse of time, and gratitude for his patience, she would marry him simply for her own comfort. She had to do something either way or lose by default.

She couldn't make the commitment. Marriage to Gary had been an unthinking college impulse squeezed in between exams — and maybe that's how all great marriages are made, she told herself. But to live with Alex the rest of her life? Maybe a year ago she would have thought her fear of betrayal, her lack of trust in those closest to her, prevented her from getting married. But that wasn't it now. She knew Alex would never hurt her.

It was simply that her need wasn't great enough; Alex was a comfortable convenience, and he was a friend.

Alex came back into the room and drank from his coffee mug. Kate had nearly finished her coffee as Alex lay down beside her.

"Now where were we, beautiful?" He kissed her ear, nuzzled into her neck, and came around to her mouth. "Um. Recall is imminent."

Kate relaxed into his kisses, the feeling of being loved, and then as his hands stroked her body, the feeling of being desired. She moved her body onto his, wrapped her arms around his head, and as she kissed his neck her body rhythmically responded to his motion.

While Alex lay in bed with a second cup of coffee, Kate put on running shorts and a nylon jacket. Alex was watching her as she bent over to tie her shoes, and she felt his eyes on her as tenderly as a caress.

"Well, handsome," she said, "you can't ride your bike from bed. Let's go." He had agreed to pace her twenty-mile run this morning.

"Give me five minutes. God, you're lovely," he added. "You go do your warmups. I'll be out in a minute."

"Do you really think my muscles need more warming up, Doctor?" Her eyes reached calmly out to his; she winked, and turned down the hall.

Kate went through the kitchen and into the garage, hitting the electric garage door opener as she entered. Grabbing Alex's ten-speed, she hit the opener one more time to close the door, and raced out with only inches to spare.

She had started into her warm-up routine before she became aware of the rain. She filled her chest with a deep

61

draft of cold air — the iciness of it invigorated the raw lining of her lungs. Exhilaration suddenly mixed with pain as the day pushed forth memory: ten years old and on Christmas vacation. They were going to the mountains for a Christmas tree. But Scott was caught smoking a cigarette and had been grounded. He'd run away. Mother got in the car to go look for him. Father would search in another direction.

Then, as now, she stood outside in a drizzling rain. Daddy called her back into the house, back into his bedroom.

Kate held her breath while all around her the day broke like splinters on her exposed flesh. She was cold.

Chapter 6

"The problem, ya know, is that I've been too sexually exclusive!" Terry announced this with the excitement of Christopher Columbus sighting land.

Angie turned on her bar stool, and listened with only half an ear. She looked around the Parking Lot lounge. It was a bit early; the faithful would not begin to crowd the bar for another hour. Maybe she and Terry should go sit out by the pool. To her still-sober nose, the smell of stale cigarette smoke and the ether-like remains of spilt beer were pungent and obnoxious.

Angie looked out the sliding glass door toward the pool. The boys were up to their usual fun. Some of them, middle-aged businessmen, drank with happy abandon, gesturing expansively, laughing good-naturedly at what seemed the slightest provocation. They were well-mannered and well-dressed, perhaps lonely, but disciplined in their daily lives. They would leave the bar at 11:00 unless they had taken a nap prior to coming in. Some men, the youngest ones, in butch haircuts and tank tops, struck sultry poses, and smiled only slightly lest a crease mar their tanned faces. They had lain by the pool all day waiting for the older man to arrive and notice them. Or anyone to arrive and notice them. Now was their time. They would go home only with the proper invitation. Nor, Angie realized from years of watching, was it money that attracted the young men. Status, good taste — but mostly it was some internal certainty these men had that the older men would care for them, father them, mentor them, and delight in them. The boys had it all worked out.

"So? It's OK with Peg if you engage in outside activities?" Although she had little contact with Terry's girlfriend, Angie liked her.

"Not exactly . . ." Terry, a study in animation, began to present her case, and Angie again listened with half an ear.

Angie smiled into the mirror across from her. She loved the bars. The first time she had gone to one, when she was eighteen, she had felt as if she had arrived in lesbian heaven. In the mid-sixties, when bars had been the only place to meet, the tension of social exchange and the emerging hippie-consciousness mixed with sexual hunger to produce an ebullience, a free expression of love, that embraced everyone. Sisterhood was in flower. Berkeley had been a marvelous place to be, and every venture into the bars had been a homecoming.

Now the bars were filled with new women. Young and arrogant, they too were discovering the mighty stimulant each was to the other. Intoxicated with alcohol and drugs, equally drunk with the tribal ritual of celebration, dancing to music amplified beyond comprehension and carried on rhythms pulsating with creative energy, one came seeking unity and left feeling not nearly so alone. Everyone found someone to hold, the details of compatibility not so much worked out as ignored. Nor did the normal impediments to social exchange matter; money, power, age, education — these didn't count. How well could you dance? How much confidence did a woman carry in her strut?

"Urumph!" Terry articulated in her morally superior Italian mother way, and played with a strand of her gray hair. "How many times you gonna let Rochelle walk out ... and beg her to return? You a goddamn ping pong ball? Fuck, she's not even our kind of people. She's not family."

"Well, fuck you very much," Angie returned primly, locking eyes with Terry's deep hazel-gray ones. "What do you mean, she's not family."

"Oh, come on. She's a thrill seeker. She's not a lesbian. She looks down her nose at all your friends. Doesn't talk with any of us. She's never too busy to warm your bed, but always, when we have a dinner or some event, then she's too busy. Listen, you want to screw with her, fine. But don't pretend this is the woman of your dreams. Honey, this woman could never be the mother of your children."

"The mother of my children? Ah, ha," Angie nodded.

She enjoyed Terry's swagger and tough talk. Terry was the only friend with whom she could be earthy, a charade they played together, mimicking the ways of their peasant grandfathers. As often as they cried over the way women in their families were treated, each in her turn could take on the mentality of her father — demeaning women, speaking harshly to each other. By mocking an ancient tradition, they purged themselves of it. Still, Angie wasn't quite in the mood for Terry's truth tonight.

Angie grabbed her beer bottle. "Besides, this is the last time. It's over."

Terry nodded, and raised an eyebrow. "Unless you got a replacement lined up, I'm willing to bet she's back in your bed . . . what? . . . two days?"

Angie admired the rise of Terry's eyebrow, the large hooded eyes which slid so easily and confidently into flirtation. With those eyes she could stop nagging parents in mid-sentence or comfort dying children who were her charges on the pediatric ward. Sometimes those eyes contained an ocean of sadness — Sisyphus rolling his rock up the mountain and following it back down — sometimes Terry was the Sisyphus, sometimes she was the caretaker of the blades of grass trampled beneath the load, sometimes in her knowledge of death she was as heavy as the rock itself. Angie respected her beauty, her humor, but most of all, her wisdom.

Tarry jabbed Angie's shoulder with a playful fist. "So, you really going to let her go this time?"

"Ah, Terry, I really feel bad," Angie conceded truthfully. "You think I'm going to let her come back." She raised her arms. "Rochelle most certainly thinks she'll be begged back. She doesn't know it won't work this time. Not this time, *poverina*." Angie shook her head, her dangling earrings bouncing emphasis. "I'm getting too old for this, you know. I need a companion, not a *donne leggere . . .*"

"Ah, so Rochelle *is* a whore?" Terry raised her eyes in knowing agreement.

"No, no!" Angie defended. "I deliberately didn't use that word. It's more like what you suggested a minute ago — she's a thrill seeker. Actually," Angie thought out loud, "she's more like an eighteenth century courtesan. She lives for grand passion and languishes in between . . ."

"*Basta!* I should be so lucky!" Terry's hands addressed the ceiling. "Peg languishes with the passion, and blooms with the in between. Wanta trade?"

"You just said Rochelle's not family. Besides," Angie feigned anger and grabbed for Terry's neck, "I'm not seeing her anymore. You notta listening to me!"

"OK," Terry laughed. "What? I'll listen."

"Well," Angie returned to her sadness, "I feel badly for her. What kind of life does she have?" Suddenly a new thought struck her, and her gray eyes grew larger. "What kind of life do *I* have, for chrissake? I'm like some kind of goddamn fifty-year-old English clerk. Getting a pot belly, knees dragging down around my ankles. No money, a cold water flat. My mistress comes in once a week to see if I can still get it up . . ."

Terry shook her head, listening attentively, apparently lost in the resonance of Angie's lament. She repeated for Angie, "Yeah, a cold water flat . . ."

"Tell me, *poverina,* why must I suffer with my women?" Angie didn't wait for an answer. "I know, I know why. It's because I don't go to Mass. God's revenge. I have to suffer through my women. That's it." Angie looked forlornly at her fingernails.

"I gotta tell you something, Lena. I take Mama to Mass every Sunday. I get two points for that — one for taking myself; one for taking Mama. But it doesn't help. God . . ." She shook her head. "He donna care about fucking. Now the Pope . . . that's a different story. He's very concerned about who's doing who." Terry swallowed her beer and ordered another round.

Angie looked at her friend seriously. "God really doesn't care?"

"What? About fucking?" Terry moved her head and shoulders to the music, snapping her fingers.

Angie nodded.

"Ah, Lena. God created Rochelle. But you're the fool who put her in your bed. The great Papa in heaven . . . he's not going to worry about a little gucchi-gucchi. You're the one who worries. Don't bother your heart."

"Gucchi-gucchi?" Angie questioned. Then she laughed. "Gucchi-gucchi! You just made that up!" Angie threw an arm around Terry.

Terry, still in time to the music, moved her shoulder into Angie's. "Wanta go make a little gucchi-gucchi?" She raised her eyes hopefully, and touched the tip of her tongue to her upper lip.

Angie nudged her body closer into Terry's, imitated her tongue motion, and picked up the rhythm of the music. "Talk me into it, woman."

"You trifle with my affections." Terry pushed her away playfully.

Angie laughed. "Only if your affections reside between your legs."

"Lena! Watch your tongue." Terry laughed, happy to see her friend in a better mood.

"Hey, Terry! Angie!" A group of women had walked into the lounge.

Angie turned and raised her beer bottle. She jumped off her bar stool, her feet unfettered by the music, and danced over to the women. In a private niche of her soul, reserved for all endings, she would continue to mourn

Rochelle until the fully experienced pain shed its skin revealing new beauty and a new beginning.

* * * * *

From the top of each earlobe he felt the need to peel off his scalp, as one would a mask, along some imaginary seam, and release the pressure, the suffocating cosmetics of a drama for which he had not rehearsed. Yet he knew what he must do for he was the son of Lightning, a true man, possessing within himself the magic of self-generation. He alone had been appointed, because of his electrical gifts, to administer shock therapy to Shewitches.

He shoved the ski mask up above his nose, and tested the night air. The heat did not bother him; it was an extension of his power. With perfect balance, taking both hands off the handlebars, he illuminated the digital read-out on his watch without, at the same time, slowing the fast pace at which he pedaled. It was three o'clock.

The night was his. All dark nights belonged to him because he alone knew how to slip through them as unperceived as gravity, as silently as still air. The swish of his bike tires left a trail of where he had been, but no one ever caught him, for the night, like a black hole in space, sucked him in to do battle with the Shewitches.

Where was the house?

He knew every inch of the bike trail. He knew every Shewitch who rode the trail; knew the patterns of all the sly women who lived within two miles of his path of light, knew when they went to work, knew when they came home. He knew who spent the night with them.

The knife wielding, castrating Shewitch chosen for him tonight had been home nearly two hours now. Alone. Now she would spend time with a real man — a man so powerful he had to stay hidden because all the black forces of Shewitches, jealous for their less manly sons, conspired to steal his weapons. They came with sirens blaring, the *weaker sons. They pretended to be the force of good; they wore badges and carried guns. He knew they were impostors sent by the Shewitches. He alone knew what was real.*

He had been led to her bedroom earlier in the evening, while she was out. The One Who Directed always pointed the correct way. In her bedroom, in his feral superiority, he had smelled her lynx odor. Yes, she was one of them, a Shewitch. She could disguise her dwelling to look like other homes — that was clever — but not her scent.

He stopped the bike, and laid it in the tall grass. Crouched, he approached the fence, lowering the ski mask, his shield, over a perspiring upper lip. Silently he slipped over the fence, and sniffed the air. His temples pounded, his eyes ached, his hands shook. Yes, the air was right. She slept.

He stood up straight, walked to the window he had opened earlier, and stood, tense as steel, listening. Within himself he gathered all the cold fury of his righteousness, of his Father's indignation. With a firm, unshaking hand he touched his genitals. Hard, stiff for battle, his electrical currents were ready. David was about to slay Goliath one more time, error vanquished, heaven vindicated.

Silently he lifted himself through the window. The true son of thunder, resplendent divinity, arched his body before the sleeping Shewitch. Fire burnt to red coals his eyes.

Vengeance is mine. Vengeance is mine.

Chapter 7

The last weekend in June had presented itself in a metallic thickness of valley pollution accented by smudged-brown skies of burn-off from the delta rice fields. But then, as the weatherman had predicted, a breeze came in through gaps in the coastal range, blowing away the pollution and cooling down the day. It had turned out to be perfect for the National Track and Field Meet to which Angie, in her Olympic fervor, had dragged Kate.

Afterwards Angie and Kate sat at a table outside an up-scale restaurant, reliving the victories of their various favorites. The emotional intensity of the day lingered for Kate. As Manning lined up on her starting blocks, Kate had crouched with her — felt blood surging through pumped up muscles, euphoria careening through the delicate wires of her brain. Concentrating, only dimly aware of the electric crowd in the stadium, she had awaited the dull crack of the gun which would signal the collision of adrenalin with time, the explosion of a perfect race. Manning flew off her blocks.

At thirty-four, each race might be her last. She had been coming in second more often than first lately. On this day, with Kate leaping from her spectator's bench, cheering from the depths of her competitor's heart, Manning conquered one more time. With tears in her eyes, Kate had felt it as a personal victory.

" 'In Xanadu did Kubla Khan a stately pleasure-dome decree . . .' " Kate held up her wine glass, proposing a toast.

"We're drinking to Coleridge?" Angie asked. Although Angie had enjoyed the day, she was especially pleased with Kate's reaction. She hadn't been sure if the Meet would depress Kate or inspire her. Clearly it had been inspirational, and Angie congratulated herself on a good idea.

"No, not Coleridge. We're drinking to all those who gather under the pleasure-dome, who drink the milk of paradise — the excellence of those who gather in the winner's circle." Kate clinked her glass to Angie's.

"And to you." Angie touched Kate's glass. "To your excellence. You have stood in that circle. Once you've stood there, I imagine you can't do less than your best or pretend you are not one of the elite. You carry it in your walk and I see it in your eyes, Katie. You're a winner."

73

"Perhaps." Kate lowered her eyes, and sipped her wine. The taste in her mouth, of garlic and salmon and lemon and chardonnay — was exquisite! She looked up, and smiled at the stars. They looked like a dispersement of glitter flung randomly by some joyous fist. A thought presented itself to her.

"So, sweetie, tell me about chaotic spikes." She smiled at Angie.

"What are you talking about, Katie?"

"It's your subject. Remember? A few weeks ago you mentioned randomness and chaotic spikes?" Mercifully, Angie had not been obsessing about the rapist lately. Kate did not want to encourage her to do so now. She wanted a nice abstract discussion.

"Oh, yeah." Angie nodded, munching on her tuna. She reached for her sparkling water. "You see, often there's no mathematical, equational differentiation. It looks chaotic. On an EEG graph, you get this line going up and up, higher than the others. There's no accounting for it, no mathematical formula for it. *That's* a chaotic spike. It's unpredictable. It's what makes human interaction so frightening sometimes." Angie was aware that she had used this model in thinking of the rapist. But she no longer felt obsessed with the rapist so she was willing to keep the conversation abstract.

"Is this something you made up?" Kate asked. "Give me a context."

"Chaos is a new branch of mathematics. You know, those people who like to account for everything with numbers and graphs. You medical people should be familiar with this stuff."

"I hope I don't regret asking this, but pray tell why?"

"Because people accord doctors all this knowledge, and doctors *believe* all their press. They think they're gods. The truth is, a good doctor can diagnose and prescribe. When it comes to attributing cause or predicting, doctors are not so great. Doctors look for similarities in bodies. They treat all bodies the same. But each body is different, and randomness plays havoc with the doctor's science."

"I don't understand the point," Kate conceded.

"I remember this story in a Kurt Vonnegut book. Two pieces of yeast were having a discussion about the purpose of life as they ate sugar and suffocated in their own excrement. Because of their limited intelligence, they never suspected that they were making champagne."

Kate laughed. "You think, Ms. Mandelli, that we humans are like the yeast?"

"Only when our arrogance robs us of compassion, and we pretend to know more than we know. For one brief moment, at creation, there was this big bang, and a huge random-looking explosion. Light and darkness exploded in varying colors —" Angie flung her arms wide, "out in every direction. If a person had been around to observe at that moment, everything would have been chaos. Then physicists came along, naming and ordering all that movement — so that it's no longer quite a mystery..."

"And if a human being lived long enough," Kate picked up excitedly, "there would be no randomness. Everything would settle into an order."

"Well, at least for doctors," Angie teased, "who have a mania for order, organization, explanation."

"But," Kate suggested, "maybe we're just imposing an artificial order because our brains have to have one. In our mania to order things, we could be ignoring other realities."

"Exactly!" Angie nearly shouted. "In our arrogance we forget that chaos is built into the universe, that predictability is only one small point on a probability curve, and that a particular explanation is only one of many."

"So what does one do? Go off looking for other realities? We lock people up for that in our society. Or," Kate thought for a moment, "we medicate them."

"You bet. Our society has a low tolerance for differences — we all have to have the same reality. But that doesn't bother me too much." Angie finished the last bite of food on her plate and thought about dessert.

"No?" Kate was curious. Surely, being a lesbian, Angie felt the effects of society's press for similitude.

"Nope." Angie smiled playfully, and winked at Kate. "This is the real joy of living. You get to let go of what other people say, and discover your own knowing."

"I don't follow you." Kate frowned.

"Well, as I see it, Dr. Ashbourne, if life is pretty random, and if memory — individual or collective — is simply a story we tell each other and not a faithful transcript of events, then we all have a lot more freedom to create our lives the way we would like them to be . . ."

"Wait." Kate held up a hand. "Now you've introduced memory . . ."

"Well, of course. In all the sense data that the world offers up to our brains, we randomly pick what to remember. Two kids growing up in the same house remember different things . . ."

"You make human psychology sound simple." Kate raised a skeptical eyebrow.

"Oh, I know it's not that simple." Angie studied the dessert menu. "An Ethiopian woman working the fields from early morning to late at night, someone striving just to get by from day to day in a third world country, may have neither the leisure nor the language to differentiate herself from her community — to think her own thoughts or run a marathon."

The waiter came and the two women decided to split a piece of chocolate cheesecake. Angie ordered a mocha coffee, and Kate an espresso.

As though never interrupted, Kate looked at Angie pointedly. "I think you're trying to tell me something, sweetie." On her elbows, Kate leaned into the table and stared across at Angie.

"You brought up chaotic spikes . . ." Angie smiled at her.

"A forty-two-year-old doctor who has the leisure to run twenty miles, certainly has the time to . . . what? . . . to write a new page in her own book?"

"To interpret her history differently, to maybe hold infinity in the palm of her hand." Angie offered as she took Kate's hand and looked directly into her eyes. "I'm not sure what is blocking you, Katie. But I know you. I know your power, your incredible strength. I see you standing underneath the pleasure-dome, in the winner's circle, and, Katie, this time I see you claiming your magic — and your prize."

Chapter 8

"Kate, I've been thinking about a puppy. What do you think?" Angie slipped her lab coat on over her light blue blouse, straightened the side zipper on her tan skirt, and admired the nice finish on her matching Botticelli heels. She was in great shape for Monday morning — and only twenty minutes late for work.

"I think that's probably something you should talk with your therapist about, sweetie. Are these obsessive thoughts?" Kate snapped some X rays off her viewing box and sipped at her coffee as she turned to face Angie.

"A watchdog, honey."

"Ah." Kate rubbed her tired eyes. Her weekly miles were beginning to take their toll; she felt exhausted all the time. To her trained mind, this indicated that she was nearing peak condition. "Are you going to stay in the cottage? An apartment is no place to raise a dog."

"Why, Katie, how could you think otherwise? I'm your coach! I need to keep an eye on you." Actually, once she had moved into Kate's cottage, Angie had not given another thought to living arrangements. It suddenly occurred to her that this might be presumptuous.

"I see." Kate felt good having Angie in the cottage. She smiled at Angie, waiting for her to continue.

"Kate, I'm working into the wee hours on your training schedule. You have no idea how much reading there is. Say —" An unconcealed enthusiasm entered Angie's voice. "— did you see where Joyce Smith won the London Marathon? She's forty-one, and has a sub 2:30 to her credit this year! She could represent England in the Olympics. Isn't that great?"

Kate's green eyes threatened a storm. "Angie, you are one of the main sources of excitement in my life — it's the rush I get at least once a week when I want to kill you." Kate didn't raise her voice.

"I'm sorry." Angie felt repentant without knowing why. "What did I say wrong?"

"England doesn't have good women marathoners. We have at least twenty-five women in this country, all under thirty, who can better Smith. Godalmighty, the Olympics," Kate mumbled more to herself than to Angie.

"Why, Katie, I'll bet you could beat Smith, too." Angie didn't skip a beat. She would not have her runner getting depressed over this thoughtless blunder. She made a mental note not to mention Joyce Smith again.

"Now that would be a good race," Kate admitted, mulling over the possibility. Then she added, "Angie, you're only two years away from forty. Don't you ever panic a little over age? Rochelle left you. You're no spring chicken."

Angie pulled at an earring, surprised that Kate had mentioned Rochelle. She wasn't ready to talk about Rochelle. Angie shook her head. "Age is appreciated in my world, Katie. Older women are in demand."

"I get it." Kate smiled, her mood lifting. "You're going to bring home a twenty-year-old, and you want a puppy to entertain her."

"*My!* Aren't we testy this morning?" Angie walked over to Kate and lightly punched her shoulder. "To tell you the truth, I was thinking I'll probably never love again, and *I* want a puppy to hug."

"I'm not enough for you?" Kate laughed, thinking that Angie had once used that line on her.

"Alex might have something to say about that." Angie had never thought about Kate sexually. To admire Kate was one thing; to desire her quite another. She quickly pushed the thought down.

For a brief confusing second, Kate almost read Angie's mind. She realized in a flash that she had been very close to feeling jealous of Rochelle, even Terry — of anyone who spent time with Angie. An athlete always bonded with her coach. It was natural. The thought fled by, and she couldn't remember what they were talking about.

"A puppy . . ." Angie answered her silent question.

"Not a big one?" Kate said hopefully.

"Nah."

"I've never had a dog," Kate pointed out truthfully.

"Dogs are gurus, Katie. They're great little beings. They mirror you perfectly. Well, sometimes that can be annoying." Angie shrugged. "You've *never* had a dog? You poor deprived woman!" She squeezed Kate's shoulder, and walked over to her files.

"How about intervals at six-thirty tomorrow morning?" Kate talked to Angie's back.

"You know we haven't talked about rent." Angie peered at Kate, ignoring her question.

"Four." Kate nodded.

"Four hundred dollars?" Angie thought that reasonable.

Kate laughed. "No, four miles of intervals."

At that moment a doctor came into the room, and both women turned their attention elsewhere.

The blue sky pierced the surrounding day with the sharpness of a mad vision. Though over sixty miles away, the Crystal Range of the Sierra Nevada Mountains, often obscured by Sacramento Valley smog, swelled before Kate and Angie in surreal nearness. The American River, all its tributaries united, rushed snow-cooled waters along the tree-lined bike trail, a twenty-six mile nature reserve. Only ten minutes into their Tuesday morning run, sweat ran down the faces of both women.

"Have you read Lyliard yet?" Angie puffed, referring to the New Zealand long-distance coach, a man who trained Olympic winners.

"No. You know I like the Oregon school of training. Prefontaine to Salazar — that's a good record."

"Always an open mind. I like that." Angie was working too hard to laugh. Maybe it was just as well, she reflected. Lyliard was into 100-mile training weeks. Kate didn't need that. She was looking a bit tired. "How many miles you doing a week now?" Angie probed.

"Fifty-five," Kate answered. "I'll be doing more," she hastened to add.

"How many?"

"Well, I've been increasing the long run by a mile every other week. Pretty conservative, don't you think?" Actually Kate had tried to increase her miles weekly. Surely the training manuals didn't refer to *her* when they talked of slow increases. . . .

Angie interrupted her thought. "No more than sixty, Katie."

"A week? Oh, come on. I figure an ultimate seventy miles a week to be really conservative. The best women in the country are doing a hundred and twenty a week. You know that."

"Katie, I'm serious," Angie said, slowing the pace in order to speak. "No more than sixty-five miles a week. Understand? You have years of running that those young women don't have. The memory of those years are in your body. You don't need the same base miles they do. They're building. You have built. That's your advantage. I wrote a letter to Dr. Sheenan. He's seventy. He should know."

"You wrote to Sheenan?" Kate was impressed at the time Angie was taking with this running business.

"Yes. No more than sixty-five a week. Promise me."

Kate was slow to answer. "I don't know."

"He runs off a base of thirty-five miles, Kate. And he breaks records." Because she couldn't use as many works as she normally did, Angie accented each with unusual deliberateness.

"Well, I am a little tired," Kate conceded. Sheenan was an expert, it was true. The man still broke age records. Maybe Angie was right.

"Orgies and drugs will do it to you." Angie remembered the second point she wanted to make.

"What are you talking about, girl?" Kate had no idea.

"Alex told me, Kate."

"Told you what?"

"About the party you went to Sunday night."

"Sweetie, sitting in a hot tub does not make an orgy. And one line of coke does not produce addiction —"

"Ah!" Angie shouted. "The logic of reefer madness!"

Kate smiled. If possible Angie was more puritanical than she. "Now, Angie . . ."

"Kate. You start out with an open mind, and end up with no mind at all. I know. I went through a brief period. Not healthy."

"You played with drugs? You hypocrite. You never told me that."

"Briefly. Five years. It's all a blurred memory." Although her tone was glib, the time she had spent on amphetamines did not please her. A pill to get up in the morning. A pill to stay up late dancing. The pace had been frantic — three hours of sleep a night. The depression she had experienced while trying to break the habit had been the lowest point in her life if only because she had lacked her normal fighting energy. Even during the break up with Sheila she had been able to lash back at the world with anger.

Kate laughed out loud. "Angie, five years is not brief. I had a marriage that didn't last that long, and it seemed eternal."

"What!" Angie grabbed Kate's shoulder. "You never told me you were married."

"You never told me you did drugs!" Kate yelled back teasingly.

83

They were running on the levee, grinding gravel underneath their feet. The river, a hundred and fifty feet to the left, meandered like their conversation and kept within the rhythm of their running. They headed for the footbridge, a miniature Golden Gate which students crossed to get from their housing to the university campus.

Several major junctions on the levee had to be negotiated — places where highways crossed the river. They were approaching one such junction. Kate loved to open up her stride on these short descents, racing downhill and underneath the bridges. Then, pumping her knees up to her chest in what was called a bounding exercise, she ascended the other side to the levee.

Rounding the corner at the bottom of such an incline, Angie keeping pace with Kate, legs stretched in full gait, they nearly collided with a biker.

"Don!" Kate exclaimed as the cardiologist swerved and lost control of his bike.

Both women ran back to the fallen biker. Don Sutherland, panting hard from the racing speed he had attained, looked up with something approaching fury in his eyes.

"Don, are you all right?" Kate bent over him. "I didn't know you took this biking business seriously. You were really moving."

"I'm fine." He jumped up, brushing her aside, and took a deep breath. "What are you idiot women doing out here at this hour of the morning? It's not even safe. For you or me. You damn runners are a safety hazard! Why do you think I have to ride this early? To avoid the runners, that's why. You stupid women! Shit!" As suddenly as his outburst started, calm returned to his voice. "Listen, hey, I don't mean to get down on you gals specifically. Just a

little on edge you know. Mendocino race next weekend."
He appended a little laugh.

"Oh, Scottie's in that," Angie exclaimed. "You know,
Kate's brother." Angie didn't know Don well, but if he
was a biker in training, she was willing to forgive his
ranting.

"Don, are you sure you're OK?" Kate asked with
maternal-medical concern. "We're on our way to the
university track for some interval work. With the speed
you came around that corner, I'd say you were doing some
intervals of your own. How fast were you going?"

"Around thirty. Your brother's Scott Ashbourne?" He
looked at Kate but didn't pause. "I didn't realize that.
He's well thought of around here. Well, listen, ladies, I
have to get to work. Patients to see, right? Have a good
run." His breathing had returned to normal, and
although his left knee was bloody, he appeared to be all
right. He jumped on his bike, and rode off without apology
or backward glance.

The women resumed their running. But Kate was
confused over the encounter. Why hadn't she known that
Don bike-raced? Alex, presently in Hawaii for a podiatry
conference, had never mentioned it. But then Alex didn't
talk much about his friends.

"God, Kate," Angie finally spoke up. "This is a violent
sport."

"You'll notice we're both fine. Looks like biking's the
sport that's dangerous."

The women started across the footbridge. It was only
6:50, but students, in mindless half-asleep disregard,
stooped under knapsacks, poked along beside them. Once
across, Kate and Angie again fell into stride. Running
through the large south parking lot, they arrived at the
track.

"Oh, damn! The gate's locked. We're going to have to climb over." Angie had noted out loud what Kate could clearly see.

"After you," Kate offered politely.

Angie took a few steps back, ran toward the chain-linked fence, jumped up and grabbed the top. Propelling her legs upward with rapid stepping motions, she balanced momentarily with both feet wobbling the fence, then leaped the six feet down, landing lightly with knees bent.

"Beautiful!" Kate admired.

"Your turn."

"It sure would be easier if our shoes fit into the links," Kate complained as she backed up to charge the fence. She accomplished the feat with as much grace as Angie.

They walked over to the track and Angie, no longer the novice, directed Kate through a series of stretching exercises until she felt that Kate was properly ready for the speed workout.

"Ready to go?" Angie took the stopwatch from around her neck. "I'll read out your quarter-mile time, and see if you can pace yourself accordingly."

"Yes." Kate, total concentration on the track, was not sure what she was yessing.

"Go!" Angie sat down, carefully watching the stopwatch, occasionally looking up to place Kate on the track. "Slow down," Angie yelled. "You'll never make a mile."

Kate ran by, and Angie yelled once again, "Too fast, one-forty seven. Thirteen seconds too fast. Pace. Pace!" Unaccustomed to raising her naturally loud voice, her vocal cords cracked. "We're not going for a four-minute mile here, Katie!"

At the end of a mile, Angie called Kate's time and instructed her to jog slowly once around the track. Five times she repeated this procedure — one fast mile, one slow jog around the track. On the last lap Kate instructed Angie to join her for one more mile.

"Come on, sweetie. You've rested long enough, and I've suffered far too long. I'll pace *you* on a seven-minute mile."

Angie joined her. Speed was a seductive mistress, and Angie, with all her recent reading, could not resist. On the last quarter-mile Kate picked up the pace even more, challenging Angie, and Angie responded so that the two women ended the run at a race. Out of breath, they bent over, panting hard, faces flushed. Kate shook out her legs while Angie walked slowly around in a bent posture.

"Not bad." Kate threw an arm around the sweating Angie. Ignoring the dampness and the clean metallic odor that accompanied it, Kate hugged her. She had suspected that Angie might have a great kick, and Angie did. "What was your time?" Kate pointed to the stopwatch in Angie's hand.

Angie looked. "Six-thirty-one!" She jumped up and hit the air with a fist. "That's great!"

"Yep! I'll bet you've got a five-minute mile in those legs." Kate felt the other woman's pride and held it gently inside herself. With just a little more work, she knew she would get Angie racing.

"I feel like I'm going to puke. Do you always feel so bad and so good at the same time?" She took a deep breath and walked to the drinking fountain.

"Only when you do your best. It's one of life's mysteries. All you need is a slow run to settle the stomach."

They rehurdled the fence and jogged slowly toward the bridge. This time it was an obstacle course filled with students. Kate, feeling protective, followed closely behind Angie. Angie, feeling the loss of intimacy in the crowd, crossed the bridge quickly. Back on the levee, no biker interrupted the flow of their stride; no noise except the crunch of gravel disrupted the contented warmth that animated their conversation.

Chapter 9

The room was perhaps thirty feet by thirty-five, Oriental in its furnishings. A thick tan and blue Persian rug ran the length of it; an off-white brocade couch faced the fireplace and separated the living room from the dining area. Pillows along the hearth suggested that this was the area in which Sheila and her friend spent most of their time. The pillows looked used. The silk screen and hanging fuchsia in crimson bloom — mirror images of Angie's — made Kate smile.

Kate thought back to when Angie and Sheila broke up. As painful as it had been then, they apparently had worked things out, down to dividing their property. Angie was the antique lover; Sheila seemed more preoccupied with textures. Yet the two had a converging simplicity in taste that had resulted in a common motif. The breakup, Kate remembered, had been caused by Sheila's desire to move. She had always wanted to live in Mendocino, and when she inherited some money, she'd made the decision. She had wanted to support Angie, allow her time to establish herself as a writer. But Angie had been unwilling to accept such an offer. Proud, Kate speculated. Or frightened. She wondered if Angie today would make the same decision. But Sheila and Angie were getting along well: Kate was surprised at Angie's attentiveness to Sheila, a side of Angie she had never seen.

A wood-burning stove near the oak table they sat around warmed them and reminded Kate that the Sacramento summers were beginning to bother her. This northern coastal village was more to her liking. The fog, lumpy as intestinal gas patterns, had trundled in earlier against an already gray sky. Now this was nice summer weather, Kate reflected. A runner's weather. The fishy smell of salt air was enough to encourage the most timid appetite — not that her appetite had ever been timid. Still, Mendocino was hospitable. A pungent whiff of garlic slid out of the kitchen as Kate sipped her red wine. She wondered what they would have for dinner, and smiled at Alex who sat in animated conversation with Angie.

"These paintings are absolutely beautiful," Alex said loudly enough for Sheila, working in the kitchen, to hear. "They soften the walls — seems to be a nice blending of the masculine with the feminine."

Kate wondered if Angie had coached Alex on this or if he had made the observation all by himself. They had never talked art before. Suddenly she felt uncomfortable for him, surrounded by women who were very definite, very sure in their respective worlds. But he looked relaxed. Kate loosened her own tension.

"Buy one, Alex!" Angie urged.

"Is there some place we can buy one of your paintings, Sheila?" Alex called into the kitchen.

"My studio, twenty feet out the back door." Balancing a large bowl of spaghetti in one hand and a basket of garlic bread in the other, Sheila laughed as she entered the room. "We could go out there right now." She looked at Angie.

"Absolutely not!" Angie jumped up and took the spaghetti from Sheila. "God, this looks just great, babe." Angie turned to Alex and Kate. "This woman makes better spaghetti than my mama."

Angie had been raised twenty miles north of Mendocino. Family dinners were always chicken and spaghetti on Sunday, and Mama smiling on proudly as her large family devastated the dining room. She spent days afterward washing the linen and cleaning up stains on the carpet. When aunts and uncles and cousins visited, it might take a week to get the house back in order, although in actuality the household was never organized. No matter. Now Mama was dead and the family scattered. But the memory of the dining table lingered — cynosure of family love.

"We'll go to the studio *after* dinner," Kate jumped in, something like alarm entering her voice at the thought of postponing dinner. She was famished — nothing unusual, but something to be taken seriously.

Sheila wore white silk pants and top, a big red sash splashed around her waist, and Kate wondered how this small woman, dripping as much gold as Angie, was going to get through spaghetti without making a mess of her

91

clothes. Not particularly taken with Sheila, Kate appraised her critically. She was too small to be pretty. As small as Rochelle. A light went on in Kate's head. Was Rochelle simply a substitute for the physical presence of Sheila? Or did Angie make a fetish of small women? Even seated, Angie loomed over this minimal woman like a giant sky. No, they definitely didn't make a good-looking couple. Angie was beautiful. This Sheila was merely . . . cute.

With half an ear Kate listened to the discussion of art — the spiritual essence of Sheila's floral cycle, the gentleness in her expression of color, Persian miniaturists, airbrushes, serigraphy, positive and negative prints. Normally interested in people and normally soft in her judgments, Kate turned her mind away from Sheila. But, she conceded, Sheila *was* a good cook. Kate admired the flavor of the spaghetti sauce, the texture of the noodles — probably freshly cooked this morning. The salad tasted of garden vegetables. Then suddenly she realized that she really wasn't hungry after all. She was tired. Probably the long drive up.

It struck Kate that Sheila was a happy woman. She wasn't faking it. Perhaps it was Angie's intensity that sometimes obscured the fact that she, too, was basically happy. All Angie's ranting and complaining were Italian theatrics, and had nothing to do with her sense of well-being. Sheila was calmer than Angie, and sat in her happiness like a friendly easy chair. In her presence, Angie seemed to soften and lose her anxious edges.

"I'll bet you're doing well financially," Angie commented to Sheila proudly. "Making enough to live on?"

"Yeah." Sheila nodded, her almond-shaped blue eyes resting on Angie. "Janet, that's my partner, takes care of all the business arrangements. Cards have been made of the prints . . . and distributed nationally as well as for our own local tourists. Right now Janet is in San Francisco with our printer, preparing for a show in Berkeley. It's nice."

"This food is delicious," Kate commented, and then noted that Angie wasn't eating. In fact, Angie's whole manner was sedate. Why hadn't she recognized it clearly before? Angie was still in love with Sheila! Jealousy? Absurd. Angie was a friend. Sheila, Kate reminded herself, had a lover. Still, put the imagination of a painter together with a writer, and fidelity probably counted for little. *They* would be concerned about beauty and romance. That was fine, Kate smiled to herself. It was not her concern. Looking at Alex, she realized that he understood the present situation between Angie and Sheila perfectly. Bless his heart. He was a sweet man.

Alex seemed to read Kate's confusion and came to her rescue. "These are great vegetables! From your garden?" He smiled at Sheila. . . .

Angie sipped her wine. She and Sheila, having cleaned up the kitchen after Kate and Alex left, now sat in front of the fireplace. Angie had known upon arrival, the moment she looked into Sheila's eyes, that Sheila was open to her. Why? she wondered. Wasn't this Janet taking good care of her? Like a knee-jerk reaction, Angie found all her protectiveness wrapping itself around the smaller woman. Yet Sheila seemed happy. Angie found herself hoping that some of that happiness had to do with her visit.

It had been three years. Sheila was more beautiful than Angie remembered. Her smallness had always been exciting, seducing Angie into a protectiveness more masculine than maternal. Of course, Rochelle was small too . . . Angie suddenly realized that Rochelle's attractiveness had been her physical similarity to Sheila.

In all fairness, Sheila had not actually left her. The breakup had hurt both of them equally — maybe Sheila more. Sheila had wanted to support her. She hadn't understood why Angie wouldn't go with her to Mendocino; why Angie valued her independence more than Sheila's love. Yes, Angie had given up a teaching position fresh out of college, and moved to Sacramento with a woman named Betty who was going to support her while she wrote. Yes, Betty had left her for another woman. Behind in a month's rent, eating peanut butter sandwiches, Angie had finally gotten the job at the hospital. "But," Sheila had argued, "I am not Betty. We've been together five years, not five months. I love you!"

But that wasn't it either, Angie could admit only now. She loved Sheila to the point of becoming lost in her — she hadn't been able to separate herself out from Sheila. Had she stayed with Sheila, she would have always stood in her shadow. That wasn't Sheila's fault, Angie knew. It was something she lacked within herself. Only in the last few years, Rochelle notwithstanding, had she come to be her own person. It hadn't been fun, but it had seemed necessary.

Angie sighed. Sheila reached across the short space that separated them and took Angie's hand. Angie turned to her, and leaning over, kissed the corner of her mouth. Sheila ran her hand through Angie's hair, and drew Angie's mouth fully to her own.

"You kiss like no other woman in the world, Lena," Sheila whispered into her ear, then nibbled around her neck. "Sometimes," she lowered her eyes, "I'm really sorry you didn't move with me. You're such a large part of my heart."

"Funny. I just realized I've spent the last year having an affair with a woman only because she reminded me of you. But," Angie held up a hand, "I didn't get lost in her."

"Were you lost in me?" Sheila frowned at her. "Really?"

"Yeah."

"Have you found your own way now?"

"I don't know," Angie answered honestly. "Perhaps. Are you happy with Janet?"

"Very much." Sheila nodded emphasis and then whispered in Angie's ear, "But I want to make love with you."

In answer, Angie drew Sheila down to the carpet. She kissed Sheila once softly, and then finding Sheila's mouth opening with her own, gave herself over to a cascade of escalating heat. Her hands, with trembling wisdom, reached underneath Sheila's blouse and felt the creamy smoothness of her breasts. Kissing her neck, Angie unbuttoned both her own and Sheila's blouse, and then looking down the length of Sheila's body, drank in her slender grace.

Sheila pulled Angie's face back to her, and in the frenzy of her own desire, licked the corners of Angie's mouth, urgently removing Angie's few articles of clothing. Their bodies surged against each other in a tide of longing and forgiveness and completeness.

Alex wore tan sailcloth pants with a multi-striped beige shirt. His watermelon windbreaker was unzipped to the middle of his ribcage. Normally most of the eyes in

95

this crowded restaurant would be on him; he was a striking man, prematurely graying at the temples, and wore his clothes as an extension of his physical grace. Or, Kate thought, all eyes would be on Angie who, when the three of them were out together, people assumed to be with Alex because they teased each other unselfconsciously and appeared to be a couple. But this morning Angie, in a swashbuckling white blouse over a pair of faded jeans, sat in understatement, playing neither fashion model nor Hollywood entertainer.

This was race day, and attention was on the racers. Scott, his second place trophy under his chair, still wore his skin-tight black racing shorts with a well-used sweat top over his racing jersey; he attracted most of the attention. As if his costume weren't enough, his matted hair and thin brown knotted legs attested to his hero's effort. People at nearby tables occasionally whispered, their heads together, nodding in his direction. Scott seemed not to notice, but Kate accepted proudly the smiles shyly offered to their table. People walking by, especially other racers, stopped to compliment him. He accepted the congratulations politely.

"Too bad you went down early in the race," Alex said regretfully, voicing what others thought. "Tough break. But second place ain't too shabby, Scott."

"The officials always check for oil. I don't know how they missed that little slick," Scott replied, his head lowered. He sipped his mineral water. "If I'd taken the same angle everyone else did, I'd have missed it." He shrugged. "The second curve on the Comptche Road — shit. . . ."

"I suppose only a spoilsport would bring the point up to the officials now?" Kate asked. She felt awful for him. Momentarily she thought of her broken arm and the

Olympics. The whimsicality of fate? Angie's theory of randomness? Or the subconscious machinations of one afraid to lose? Or afraid to win? Maybe it ran in the family. Scott had lost it on a curve. She had simply fallen down a flight of stairs.

"Yep." Scott nodded emphatically. "I should have been paying more attention."

"Isn't that the way most races go?" Angie felt too subdued to talk but she cared too much for Scott not to join in consoling him. "You go through all the preparation, all the training. Then comes race day and you pull a muscle or run into an oil slick or torrential winds come up . . . all the training comes to nothing. But still, it takes courage to get up and keep doing your best, Scott. Second is a good finish. You've won before and you'll win again."

"Oh, sure. I guess." His shoulders still sagged.

"We're proud of you, Scott," Alex put in.

The food arrived. Kate looked at her crab omelet, and realized she was famished. Angie eyed her strawberry omelet with great interest, looking at Kate, and smiled happily.

"Got your appetite back, sweetie?" Kate questioned her favorite eating companion.

"Possibly. I don't know whether to attack my plate or Alex's sausages first." Through a haze of contentment, Angie looked at Kate, and realized with some alarm that this morning Kate seemed desirable. What's the matter with me, she wondered. Maybe Sheila woke up a sleeping libido.

"I would never have guessed that a little love could tone you down so much," Kate teased.

"Don't remind me." Angie lowered her eyes, embarrassed at her own thoughts. "This omelet might go to waste."

Kate listened to the continuing conversation at the next table. A group of three women and one man were talking about some calamity of the previous night.

"Right out there on the bluffs . . . just down this road." A woman in a green polyester blouse gestured out the window.

"And she's still alive!" marveled a woman in a 1950s-style rhinestone-studded glasses.

"Paralyzed from the waist down," the balding man said with assurance.

"When did all this happen," Alex mumbled to Kate. "Surely it's too early for such a diagnosis and prognosis." Kate smiled at him and he returned her smile. They made a game of quietly commenting on other people's conversation.

"Just imagine!" exclaimed the lady in green. "All these people in town for that race, and there's some psycho out walking the bluffs at night. We should leave this morning, really!"

"Oh, Rita, just think. He tied her hands and raped her and threw her off the cliff — my, the world we live in!"

"Maybe she can identify him," Rita hopefully suggested.

"It was so dark," the man answered practically.

"Are you listening, sweetie?" Kate looked at Angie.

"It's a race to see if I can finish my food before the subject kills my appetite." Angie looked at Kate with an expression meant to convey that her question was foolish. But since her nightmare and the phone call to Nunzio, thoughts of the rapist bothered her less.

"Well, it just isn't Sacramento." Kate sighed.

"That's not terribly comforting, Katie. I'm supposed to sleep better because the *whole* world's crazy?" Angie smiled at her teasingly.

"At least I didn't lose the Derosa," Scott said absently, in reference to his bike.

Alex changed the subject. "Too bad Sheila couldn't join us."

"When a paint brush calls . . ." Angie replied. "I love the painting you bought, Alex. A man of discriminating taste."

"How's Don?" Kate addressed Alex; he had gone over to talk with his friend Don Sutherland after the race.

"So disgusted with his showing he wouldn't join us for breakfast," Alex answered.

"Fifteenth isn't so bad in a field of three hundred." Kate shook her head in disbelief. Nevertheless, as a competitor, she knew how both Don and Scott felt, and that anything less than first place always hurt.

Chapter 10

"Suggest recheck in three months to rule out . . ."

Angie, her work done for the day, waited for Kate to finish dictating. She briefly considered driving to San Francisco for a Scandinavian art show, then decided to use one of her vacation days next week for that. It would be fun to go with Rochelle; the woman really understood art. But that was out. Rochelle, after calling several times, had finally gotten the message that Angie was no longer interested. She hadn't called in several weeks. A friendship with her was out of the question, Angie lamented. After Rochelle had hooked her sexually, she had even stopped talking art. No, the relationship had never been built on friendship.

Maybe she should go to the basement lounge and touch up her fingernail polish. Nunzio might go to San Francisco with her. She was on vacation all next week and Nunzio was driving up to spend time with her.

She sighed. When would Kate be done? She needed to discuss training with her. No one appreciates the sacrifices a coach makes, she thought in her mother's voice, and smiled, recognizing the voice of her own mother.

Angie had subscribed to every running magazine in the country. Read Jim Fixx. Studied diets — but Kate ate so much of everything she had all those bases covered. She studied training schedules and read every interview any Olympian gave. With the dedication of the born historian, she liked to research a subject completely.

Too bad Terry was in New York. Terry always went shopping with her on payday nights. A new pair of spectator pumps would be nice. Irwin's was having a big sale. A new burgundy leather bag. A new slip. Now that's what she needed. Something frilly. She realized that she was thinking of her favorite things just to avoid thinking of her book. Once she got into thinking about her book, she wouldn't be able to concentrate on anything else, and there was this running business to get straightened out with Kate.

Kate returned some X rays to their jackets and turned to her. "Are you waiting for me, sweetie?"

"Patiently." Angie nodded wide-eyed. "I need to talk with you about the Galloway Running Clinic. Ever heard of it?"

"No," Kate answered thoughtfully. "But Jeff Galloway won the ten-K in the Olympics several years back..."

"*That* Galloway Running Clinic," Angie cut in excitedly. "He goes all over the country putting on clinics. He'll be at Tahoe, Olympic Village, in September. I think it would be a good idea for you to go."

"Absolutely not!"

"What?" She hadn't expected Kate to jump with joy at the idea, but this strong negative reaction surprised her. "You have something against Galloway?"

"No, of course not." Kate laughed, as surprised as Angie at her response. "I don't need instruction. God, Angie, I've been running for thirty years. Nor do I want to draw attention to myself by going to something like that."

"Ah, the true extrovert. Listen, if you do this, I promise not to take out the full front page ad I was going to buy in support of your efforts. I was thinking we could turn out most of Sacramento to watch you run..."

Kate glared at her.

"I've been querying *Running Times* and *Running World* to see if they might be interested in an exclusive interview. Maybe *Sports Illustrated.*"

"Enough." Kate held up her hand. "What's your price?"

"The Running Clinic, Katie. Lyliard will be there. I know you don't think much of him, but he's produced some great winners. They'll do videos of your running, Katie, and critique your form. Important. They'll give you a personally designed running schedule for peaking just before the marathon. Important. But most important, you'll get some altitude running. Think of your increased oxygen uptake. A week at Tahoe, just concentrating on running — I highly recommend it."

"This isn't a recommendation. This is blackmail."
Kate frowned. In a swing of memory, she thought back to
the coaching she had had in high school — all the
criticism engineered for improvement, the stingy praise
and mind-numbing work. Suddenly Angie sounded like a
real coach, nit-picking for the thirty second edge or the
half second that distinguishes the winner from the losers.
Increased oxygen uptake!

Kate knew the will to win closed off all other
possibilities, zeroed in like a microscope focus, everything
in life becoming subordinate to the commitment. She
found herself wavering, not wanting to make the
commitment for fear of appearing ridiculous. Maybe
Angie was just a silly, enthusiastic child, an extension of
her own foolishness.

Kate shook her head at Angie who sat waiting for an
answer. Maybe this self-questioning was merely an
expression of fear. Kate touched the tip of her nose with
an index finger. Maybe Angie was waiting to see a real
commitment. Afraid of losing, Kate needed to believe that
she could win, and in order to believe that, she had to do
all she could to prepare. Damn Angie! Sneaking around
only half-committed was the safest way to approach
anything; Angie with her undisguised enthusiasm clearly
did not recognize the virtue of fence-sitting.

"Listen, sweetie, instead of that, I was thinking of
running in the Oakland Marathon. Use it as pre-peaking
indicator." Kate casually touched the bun on the nape of
her neck, checking for loose hairs. "It would help my
pacing —"

"Help your pacing!" Angie's voice cracked. "It would
ruin your pacing! You'd get sucked right into the race,
lose your head and go for the win. Do I look stupid, Kate?
The Oakland Marathon would blow your entire training.

You don't have to go out there and see if you still know how to run, you *know* how. all you've been talking about lately is a fun run. You're looking for an excuse to race — to make sure you haven't forgotten. Kate! I promise you, you still know how to race. Don't you dare sneak a race in on me."

Kate laughed, a little embarrassed. She wanted nothing so badly as to test her training, and feel the instant gratification of victory. Angie was right. "When's the clinic?" she asked.

"Third week in September." Angie's eyes danced. "You going?"

"I won't go for the entire week."

Angie pulled at an earring. "You could go for three or four days."

"Okay. If you register me for four days — two of those on the weekend — I'll arrange for us to get the time off. You *are* going, right?"

"Oh, sure," Angie was surprised to hear herself say. She needed the time for research . . . Well, she could take some books with her. Maybe throw in one or two on coaching.

"One other thing, Mandelli. I absolutely want to race and win the Badger Hill five miler. It's *only* five miles, in the mountains for oxygen uptake." She raised an eyebrow to Angie. "And good hill work. I can treat it like an interval workout. Okay?"

"Okay," Angie conceded graciously. Five miles *would* be a good distance, an interval workout. At least Kate wasn't suggesting anything over that distance. "We'll go for a 6:15 mile pace on it."

"A flat six, sweetie."

Angie changed the subject. They could negotiate the pace later. "Want to go shopping after work? Say, is that a little muscle I see?" Angie pointed to Kate's sleeveless arms.

"The workouts at the health club are paying off, don't you think?" Kate felt pleased that Angie had noticed, but she returned to the first question. "I thought you and your Italian buddy Terry went shopping on paydays." Kate liked Terry. She was droll. Besides, she had a reputation as an outstanding nurse; the doctors spoke well of her.

"Terry's in New York. Her father's in the hospital. He's seventy-two. Kidneys."

"Oh, I'm sorry. Sure, let's go shopping." Kate didn't feel much like shopping, but if that's what Angie wanted to do . . ."

At that moment a Code Blue came over the intercom. Someone in the X ray area had stopped breathing. Kate bolted out of her chair. In the hallways, if procedures were being followed, two other doctors and three nurses were rushing in the same direction.

* * * * *

The voice in his ear chilled him, turning the rivulets of sweat running down his arms and back into streams of icy water. The hair stood up on his arms. He pulled the blanket up around his neck.

Why? he asked. Why? He did not mean to be impertinent. He had never questioned the Director before. Even when the Director woke him in the middle of the night and told him to go, unprepared and unknowing, out into the night — he did not question. He trusted.

But this? It was a new message.

"Prepare the rod. Prepare to kill."

Had he understood correctly? Was this a new message? Was it an old message in a new form? What was expected of him?

He would wait out the night without sleep. He would wait for the voice, for clarification. He would know, as he knew all, as the One Who Directed knew all.

He stared as the mosaic of the room blended through the contours of his mind, projecting back out a shadow-show of meaning on the ceiling.

Chapter 11

Kate, in a pair of yellow shorts and a T-shirt, lay on the couch, her tired legs propped up on its arm. Her twenty-four mile run done, she looked forward to maintaining her present position for the rest of the day, an occasional trip to the well-stocked refrigerator the only concession to mobility she might make. Alex was at a friend's cabin, helping to chop wood for winter. He wouldn't be back until noon tomorrow.

She looked contentedly around the immaculate spare bedroom which she had converted to a family room. The cleaning lady came on Fridays, and Kate was pleased with the arrangement; she could live in a clean house on the weekend. Although neither she nor Scott cluttered, a freshly vacuumed house *smelled* clean. She picked up a current issue of *The Journal of American Medicine,* and leafed through it. Looking forward to the spy novel on the floor, first she had to pay homage to her profession.

A car approached outside, and Kate held her breath, waiting for it to drive by. The car stopped. Across the street, she thought hopefully. Moments later the doorbell rang. Kate toyed with the idea of not answering the ring, but it might be a friend of Scott's. Reluctantly she put her legs on the floor, groaning as she propelled herself into motion and shuffled off to the door.

"Katie, dear," her mother chirped. "Your father said last night, 'Let's go visit friends in Sacramento and see the children.' Such a marvelous idea, we took the first plane out this morning, rented a car, and here we are, we'll stay in a hotel although Sacramento doesn't offer much in that department. Your father wants to make sure the house is okay, that the pruning gets done correctly, isn't that right, Charles?"

Plump and gray-permed, expensively tailored as always, her mother turned to her father, equally well groomed but looking more overweight than when Kate had seen him last — three years ago at Christmas. "And we have many other friends here to visit so you don't have to drop anything to entertain us, just go on about your business like we're not even here, we realize you may have other plans. In fact, I'm rather surprised to find you home. It was just an impulse, isn't that right, Charles?"

Her mother came up for air but did not pause. "Although I can't imagine you'd be going out dressed like that. Oh, I know, I'm so old-fashioned, I see it all the time, women go grocery shopping, even browse in department stores dressed in sweatpants, but I know no daughter of mine would do that — such a bad reflection on one's up-bringing. Is your brother home?" She came to an abrupt halt.

Oh, fuck! Kate tried to clear the frown from her forehead as she searched for a smile. "Mom, Dad." She hugged her mother, turned, and hugged her father. "Come in, come in." She tried to sound enthusiastic even while the first wave of shock receded, while she wondered how she had happened in a matter of seconds to walk from a soft couch into a bad dream.

What would she do with her parents? Her parents! She was far too tired to maintain any semblance of consciousness, and she knew from past experience that handling her mother required superhuman alertness. Her mother's tedious adventures into meaningless conversation invited inattentiveness; yet at the same time, if she so much as nodded assent at the wrong moment, her mother could have her on the next plane to Paris for a little shopping. Her father, on the other hand, would sit, his eyes brightly lit — perhaps a technique he developed early in their marriage — and look the picture of studied interest. He daydreamed, Kate knew. Perhaps of murder. He liked old Hitchcock movies. He was masterful at avoiding substantiality, of avoiding anything that gave off the medicinal odor of reality; conversations that required any decision he considered contradictory to his fantasies, his private mental health pharmacy. Mom and Dad were well suited.

"You must have some luggage. Let me call Scott. He's in the backyard."

Kate dashed off through the house. Scott would not be pleased, she thought in supreme understatement, avoiding her own anger. If she tolerated her parents, Scott

109

avoided them. The only times she had ever seen him lose patience, became angry to the point of incoherence, were in connection with their mother who responded by pampering him as if he were an incompetent child. Usually he disappeared when his parents were near; simply left without a word. But Kate would not allow that this time. She was too tired to deal with her parents alone. Although, she thought parenthetically, it's a good thing I'm tired. Exhausted really. Otherwise, I'd kill them. No, Scott would have to stick this one out with her.

How did her parents get off just dropping in like this? They had never before done such a thing. If they had, Kate reflected grimly, such visits would become the nightmare material of her sleeping hours. Even her waking hours. Her mother approved of nothing she said or did. God, Kate told herself, if she knew I was practically living with a man, she'd move to Sacramento to protect my virtue. Well, I'd move to Timbuktu and leave no forwarding address.

Her mother had always disapproved of Kate's running. Too masculine. Bad for a woman's body, she had insisted against all contrary evidence. Being a doctor was wrong too. Kate had gone to medical school without her mother's approval. Her father, ignoring his wife's objection for perhaps the first time in his life, had paid Kate's tuition. It was the most courageous thing he had ever done as far as Kate knew, and probably he had done it out of guilt.

Kate swallowed her disgust. She could almost forgive her father — no matter how misguided, he had loved her. But her mother! Three years of therapy, and still her mother could plug her in like a light bulb. Seventy dollars an hour, and still she was salivating like Pavlov's dog when her mother punched a button. *Damn!*

Scott saw her and turned off the lawn edger. "Have you seen the new guard dog?" He strode toward her, wiping his hands on his tattered cut-offs, a broad smile on his handsome face.

Kate ignored his question, took him by the arm and led him toward the house. Plunging into the immediate problem she said, "Have I got a surprise for you. Dust yourself off and come with me, brother." She turned and faced him. "And let me tell you right off, I'm tired and can't begin to handle this alone. Please don't desert me. Mom and Dad are here."

Without a word, as though Kate were not even present, he turned on a bare foot, and headed for his side of the house. Kate, in quick sureness, grabbed his arm, spun him back on track. "No, Scott. This way."

"Did you know they were coming?" His jaw was clamped in rigid tension, his eyes had glazed over.

"Absolutely not!" Kate emphatically answered while firmly leading him by the arm through the house. She felt the hardness in his arm muscles, knew that any second he might bolt. Dear God, she thought, I *am* going to have to handle this by myself.

When Scott saw his parents his mouth gaped open and then slammed shut. He spoke not a word; he paled. Kate, her arm through his, her hand on his wrist, felt his pulse race, and knew that adrenalin gushed through his body like water through an uncapped water hydrant. This was a family neurosis, she told herself, non-delirious madness.

His mother raced to him. "Scottie, baby!" She clung to him, patting his head, straightening his hair, fidgeting over his clothing. "Baby, the house really does need another coat of paint, your father and I were just this moment discussing it. You two working people, why you could afford to have someone come in and paint. You may

111

have to budget for it, but we feel the responsibility is yours now, it would do you and your sister good to plan such things together. It doesn't look like either of you will marry though perhaps it's too soon to make that prediction. You remember that nasty girl you were dating? I told you she was no good, and I was right, better not to marry at all. I only want to spare you pain. Baby, your jeans are torn. What have you been doing? Oh, yes, Kate said you were in the backyard. Mowing the yard? My, such a man! You father's going to help you prune the trees. Isn't that right, Charles?"

"Stop it!" With two trembling hands, Scott took his mother's caressing fingers and flung them from the front of his T-shirt. "This is not the right fucking time to prune. You know that, Dad." His voice sounded nearly normal.

Kate quickly removed her arm from his, but felt him sway. She hadn't realized how he had been leaning on her. Taking a step backward, she had the sensation of viewing this family scene through rising gasoline fumes, wiggly and out-of-focus and just faintly noxious.

Her father nodded at Scott, concentration etched across his face; but his eyes failed to register comprehension. Kate wondered if his hearing was getting worse. His deafness, the result of a fungus contracted during the war, probably had saved his marriage; but Kate, in a surge of pity, couldn't imagine that it was a marriage ever worth saving. Besides, it was hard to deal with a man who cultivated his handicap like a rose garden, a built-in thorny defense against the world. God, he was a weak man, and although there might be some good explanation, in pity and repugnance she would never respect him.

Her mother came to Charles' defense. "Of course, Scottie, of course, your father knows when it's time to prune. But he can show you how, isn't that right, Charles?" She continued to address Scott, "Baby, you look so pale, are you all right? Your sister the doctor doesn't even notice. Have you been taking care of your brother, Kate? He doesn't look well. Oh, you two probably party all night now that no one is around to watch you. Children have no sense, you both should have a family, some responsibility, it matures you, it's healthy. I bet your sister doesn't even cook for you, baby. Not your sister. She knows how to operate but not how to cook like a decent woman. A woman should cook and do the laundry and take care of her brother, Kate. This doesn't even look like a true home to me, just a place where you two sleep . . . sometimes. Now I know men have urges, but there is no excuse for you, Kate."

Thinking only of the turbulence in her stomach, Kate blurted, "Scott only got pale when he heard *you* were here, Mother!"

Kate suddenly felt doomed. She had never talked back to her mother. Not once. Death could not be this painful. But even as a wall broke inside, she looked her mother fully in the face, did not look away.

Nothing happened. Silence filled the room. Scott's mouth quivered in a smirk.

"Nonsense!" her mother finally pronounced. "Charles, did you hear how your ungrateful daughter just insulted us?" She raised her voice in a true effort to break her husband's hearing barrier. "We send her to medical school and this is the way she repays us . . ."

She continued the lecture, but Kate, like her father, shut her out. Surely any minute Scott would leave — she could see the vein standing out in his throat, beating against his tan neck. Through the living room window she saw Angie drive up in her ancient Porsche, the car disappearing in the driveway along the side of the house. She had to decide what to do with her parents.

Scott interrupted his mother. "I'm going to work in the backyard."

"Kate, you're not taking care of him —"

In the tension of her mother's face Kate perceived a smugness, and she suddenly suspected that it had been her intention all along to drive her son away. A line from the poem raced through her mind: *Families are a breeding-ground for scorpions . . .*

"— he is such a delicate child. You should be doing the yard work. He works hard all week. You just sit in an office. Your brother nearly died of asthma —"

"His last attack was the night of high school graduation, Mother. When you re-dressed him three times before he left, and told him his date was unsuitable. That was the last time . . ."

"You're lying —"

"No she's not!" Scott's face was red. Raising his arm, his body trembling, he looked as though he might strike his mother. Instead, he turned and left the room.

"Now look what you've done, Kate! You've upset your brother —"

"Mother!" Her voice was quivering, she knew her face was red. "I want you and father to leave. You cannot come to our house uninvited and unannounced. You have no right. I want you out! Now!" Her voice automatically knew what to say as her mind, groping toward survival, failed to register the words. She pointed at the door.

"Kate, don't talk to your mother that way." Unaccustomed as her father was to using his voice, his words fell flat.

"Out!" Kate shouted.

"This is not your home, lady." Her mother's whisper was a snarl. "Your father and I still own this house. You live here by our good graces, you ungrateful child."

"You can take this house and shove it." Kate heard herself say the words calmly, and the confidence of her authentic voice echoed in her ears. She felt as though she were on the top of a cliff, ready to fly. "Ungrateful? You listen. Your husband, the man you married, molested me. *Me,* your nine-year-old daughter, while you were busy avoiding both of us, working your sickness on Scott —"

"She lies —" Her mother covered her ears.

"You," Kate continued, raising herself onto the balls of her feet and staring down at her mother, "you never protected me, defended me, mothered me. You fed me, and you made me tough. For that I am not grateful. For none of it. Get out. *Out!*"

Kate moved toward her mother who stood with her hands still over her ears. Her father moved between them, and took his wife by the arm.

"Come, Margaret." He gently led her to the door. "We'll come back when Kate is feeling better. This is not a good time."

The door, like a gaping wound, stood open. Kate slowly walked to it. With all her new-found strength she slammed it shut. With her back to the door, she slid to the floor. She laughed. How simple it was.

She got up, walked to the bathroom, and vomited.

Kate knocked at the cottage door. Angie quickly answered it, stepping outside.

115

"Shhh." Angie placed one finger over her lips, then noticed the six-pack of LaBatt's ale in Kate's hand. "She's napping."

"Who's napping?" Kate whispered earnestly.

"Sophie." Angie smelled the beer on Kate's breath. It occurred to her that Kate might be tipsy. Breaking training, she thought sternly. Oh, well, a beer sounded good. She took the six-pack from Kate and removed two beers, handing Kate one.

"Is Sophie someone you brought home last night?" Kate accepted the beer. "An old love, a new love, and poof, no more Rochelle? You ladies of Lesbos can be so decadent. Want to sit down?" Kate indicated the lawn. "Scott did a nice job today. Wonder where he went."

Kate knew she was chattering; she felt immensely light. Before, her parents had always threatened to leave over some imagined slight; she had always placated them, insuring that they would stay. But this time she had actually thrown them out! Their departure contained meaning and consequences yet to be measured. She drank in celebration.

Angie latched onto a possible criticism and set the record straight. "Katie, I am not decadent." Kate must be drunk. She never put that many non sequiturs into one short speech. Angie smiled. What the hell, she was a new mother and could afford to be generous. "Sophie is our new watchdog."

"Our watchdog is napping? Hardly an auspicious beginning."

"She's resting up for the night," Angie defended.

Kate changed the subject. "What are you doing for the rest of the evening, sweetie? I would like your company. Are you busy?

116

"Katie, I'm a new mother. I have to stay home and take care of baby." Angie felt confused. Kate was never this direct. Something was wrong but something was right, too. She wondered about the car in the driveway earlier, and she was still curious about Scott. Shortly after she had come home, Scott had rushed outside, picked up the lawn edger, smashed it across a tree. He had then neatly picked up the pieces and disappeared around the side of the house. "Something's going on around here, Kate. Want to tell me about it?"

"Oh, nothing's going on." Kate brushed aside the question more out of years of conditioned reticence than any sense of intrusion. "Want to order a pizza?"

"Sure! A large combination. Come on in. But be quiet. She's napping, remember." A few more beers and she'll tell me what's wrong, Angie assured herself.

Kate picked up the beer, and they walked into the house. She tiptoed to the refrigerator door, put the beer inside, and then studied the contents with an expression as serious as a student reading the cabala.

"Are we going to get drunk tonight?" Angie whispered across the kitchen, phone in hand, ready to place the pizza order. "Do we have something to celebrate? I'll have them put candles on the pizza and order more beer."

"Yeah, order more beer," Kate whispered back and decisively took another beer out of the refrigerator.

"Who belonged to the car today? The one in the driveway?" Angie asked as they sat on the floor in front of the couch.

"That's a dog?" Kate's face lit up as she pointed to the contents of a cardboard box.

"That's Sophie," Angie announced proudly, unable to contain her enthusiasm any longer. She lifted the small animal out of its box. "We have to go outside and go to the bathroom now."

"Angie!" Kate laughed delightedly. "When I said no large dogs I didn't mean you should get something half the size of an atom. This little hairy particle couldn't protect you from an ant." She followed Angie outside. The day was cooling down nicely. The breeze felt good.

"You jest now, Katie, but in a week we'll have a tiger on our hands. I know how to pick a dog. She's got a potential bark that will knock your socks off. Believe me."

"Okay," Kate agreed. "What is it?"

"A dog!" Angie shouted indignantly.

Kate punched Angie playfully. "My, aren't we defensive. What *kind* of dog, silly?"

"Oh." Angie, embarrassed, lowered her eyes. "She's a Yorkie. Oh, look Kate! She's peeing! Isn't that something?"

"I'm impressed."

"Ah ha. Well, just wait until she poops." They both laughed. "Good girl, Sophie." Angie picked up the limp bundle and cradled her.

Kate stood a respectful distance away, took a swig of beer, and eyed the new watchdog. "Can we expect Sophie to become more than six inches tall?"

"*Possible.*" After placing Sophie back on the grass, Angie straightened her Anne Klein short-sleeved blouse.

Kate sat down on the grass and picked up the dog. "My God, you're soft." Sophie opened both eyes and stared at Kate with vulnerable defensiveness. "Oh, you're a cutie all right, but your name is bigger than you are." Sophie nipped at Kate's neck.

"Pretty great, huh?" Angie asked. "Just right for the cottage."

"Honey, if you had gone out for an alarm system, you'd have come back with a bell —" Kate laughed lightly and kissed the dog's head. "Sophie's starved, incidentally. I can spot hunger a mile away . . ."

Two hours later Angie walked to the refrigerator for another beer, and came back to look at the nearly demolished pizza on the coffee table. She giggled. Not able to keep up with Kate in the drinking department, she nevertheless felt relaxed and happy.

"Think we should give Sophie some?" Kate asked, eyeing the sleeping dog at her feet.

"Might be too rich. Besides, we don't want to start her out on any bad habits."

"Right. In another hour we'll be resty for the ready." Realizing immediately what she had said, she laughed at the spoonerism.

Angie laughed too, and then frowned as a new thought struck her. "Katie, we're setting a bad example for the little one here. Her first memories will be of beer breath. I can see her in puppy school now, complaining of her alcoholic mother. This won't do."

"Angel, I'd exchange either one of my parents for two alcoholics any day."

"*That's* who was here today!" Angie slapped the palms of her hands together.

"Yep. So you want to know what gives with my family? It's not pretty." Kate got up and weaved her way into the kitchen for another beer. When she returned she sat on the floor close to Angie. She did not speak.

"So what gives with the folks?" Angie prompted.

Kate looked intently at her beer bottle. "The long and short of it, my father molested me." Kate hung her head.

119

"He always waited for mother to leave, which she did frequently, and then he would call me into their bedroom. Made me undress . . ." Kate shook her head, trying to rid herself of the image. She straightened her head. "You can't imagine what a relief it was to discover track. I stayed away from home as much as possible."

"Oh, Katie." Angie put the palm of her hand to her head, all her rape crisis training as a counselor racing through her head. She put an arm around Kate, and tears came to her eyes. She swallowed hard. "I know you've seen a therapist. You've referred to that in the past. Did you get this stuff worked out?"

"Who knows?" Kate's chin started to tremble. "I thought so. I've studied all the literature, you know. Read everything. I'm a doctor, remember? It really isn't so uncommon —"

"Oh, Christ, Katie!" Angie interrupted. "That doesn't make it any easier, saying it's not uncommon. Statistics don't heal your heart!" Angie took Kate's chin in her hand and placed her cheek next to Kate's. "Now does it?"

Kate turned her head and swallowed. "I kicked them out of the house today. I did that!" She nearly yelled at Angie. Tears filling her eyes, she turned back to Angie. "I feel so . . ." She groped for words.

"What? What do you feel?"

She took a deep breath, the tears rolling down her cheeks, and answered, "I feel alone."

Angie stroked her hair, and wiped the tears away with her thumbs. She rubbed her back. Kate crumpled in her arms, and Angie rocked her. After a while the sobbing diminished, then stopped. Angie continued rocking her for a long time.

"Kate?" Angie whispered into her ear. There was no response. Angie gently pushed her back against the couch.

"Well, we can't have her drunk-walking back to the house, now can we?" Angie addressed Sophie. "Besides, I think she's out."

Angie lifted Kate by the shoulders, and dragged her into the bedroom. Undressed her. Folding down the sheets, she tucked Kate in. She patted Kate's head, and resisted the urge to lean down and kiss her.

After taking Sophie outside one last time, Angie kissed the dog's head and placed her in a box next to the bed. She undressed and tumbled down next to Kate. She was asleep in seconds, her brain anesthetized as completely as a body under a surgeon's knife.

Angie got up once during the night to take Sophie out. Returning to bed, she felt Kate's body cuddle into hers. Briefly Angie considered sleeping on the couch. She didn't have the strength to move.

Chapter 12

Kate awoke with the need for water stronger than the need to use the bathroom. Where was she? This was neither her bedroom nor Alex's. She turned over, coming nose to nose with Angie. She suppressed a giggle. These wild nights must cease, she thought.

As she headed for the kitchen, the events of the preceding day rushed over her. She felt only relief — that her parents were gone, that she had confided in Angie. In fact, she felt great. Opening the refrigerator, she was delighted with the quart of sparkling water that presented itself.

As she entered the bedroom from the bathroom Angie, eyes half-opened, asked, "Will you throw Sophie out for her morning job, Kate?"

Kate scooted the tan dustmop out the front door, returned to the bedroom, and got back underneath the sheet. Feeling the need for more sleep, she was grateful for the shuttered darkness of the room she had remodeled last year. She had spared no expense, and now because Angie had the cottage, she was glad she had spent the extra money.

"I better feed her," Angie groaned as she got out of bed.

"Motherhood a burden already?" Kate teased. Angie, eyes nearly closed, peered at her. Kate turned over and shut her eyes. She was happy she had done her long run yesterday. The morning was hers for sleeping.

Angie returned. She moved the edge of her pillow into Kate's back, put an arm over Kate just below her breasts, and positioned her knees up into Kate's legs. Kate was startled but pleased at the same time — the warmth felt good, the lingering remnants of Angie's perfume smelled pleasant. Yet she was aware of her own shallow breathing, and her heart pumped rapidly. She felt compelled to say something.

"Sweetie, what do you think you're doing?"

"What?" Angie feigned sleepiness. Too late, she realized what she had done, and now she didn't know how to extract herself. She didn't *want* to extract herself. The sweet smell of Kate's body swept through her — this was not what she had intended when she'd cuddled up. God in heaven, what was a lesbian to do? By some warped divine sense of humor, through no act of seduction, a beautiful woman graced her bed! And it was her best friend! What would Sappho do? Now her body was totally awake. Damn!

Angie thought carefully. She did not want to scare Kate away. She admired Kate, adored her really. Let's face it, Angie grimly admitted, I'm crazy about her. But she's a heterosexual with a very real boyfriend. Rochelle's husband she hadn't known about until late in the affair or she would have never gone to bed with her either. Terry and she were of the same mind on this subject — you didn't go outside of family, into the heterosexual world, for a partner. But now what? Kate was already in her bed. She didn't want to embarrass both of them, possibly hurt their friendship. With the intuitive sensitivity of a woman whose sexuality is intertwined with other women, Angie knew when a woman was vulnerable. Kate was vulnerable. Kate would not refuse her. But that would be taking advantage of a friend.

Okay, Angie told herself. Let's put down our guard and be honest about this. It's not a quick one-time thing I'm looking for. I want to wake up to Kate every morning. That's a problem.

Angie gritted her teeth. I'm in love with this woman. I've been in love with this woman for a long time. Right before my very eyes, I've been courting her for four years! Where *have* I been? Well, she answered her own question facetiously, I've been running around the streets of Sacramento half-naked with this woman at 6:30 in the morning. When was there time to notice?

No, Angie corrected herself, noting that Kate had not moved. It was because of Rochelle. Rochelle had filled her sexual needs, and Kate had been her companion. Fool! She had divided her life like half of the heterosexual women in the world. No more, she told herself. She would correct this situation. But not now. The next move was up to Kate.

Kate, her eyes closed, concentrated on breathing slowly. Angie's body felt like a furnace. Think, she ordered herself. They had always touched each other. She enjoyed Angie's touch. Now Angie only had an arm over her. This was not a sexual advance. Angie had never once made any kind of sexual advance — there had never been so much as an innuendo. She was making too much out of nothing. Ignore it.

No, she couldn't ignore it. With the clarity and honesty of a woman who had cleared all her accounts the day before, she knew she must face this. She and Angie played well together, worked well together. They had a closeness more intimate than any she had ever known. From deep within, she felt a maternal fullness that suddenly made her fearful for Angie — not that Angie was in danger — no, just an anxious, nameless caring that wanted to wrap this child in a womb-like world, there to minister to her needs, her hungers, to give joy that no harsh reality could encroach upon. She wanted to touch Angie, feel her substantiality, know that she was safe. Kate felt an ache inside, deeper, less urgent than pain, gushing with the same warmth as menstrual blood. This was desire she had never felt before, and she knew there was no other name for it — desire.

Oh, God! Kate shook herself mentally. Does this mean I'm a lesbian? No. No. It's just Angie. I love *her.*

Ah ha, a voice inside her smiled. Sure. You love this woman, and you desire her. When other women feel that, they're lesbians. When you feel it, it's some mysterious heterosexual twist of fate. Breathe, Ashbourne. Breathe.

Kate turned over onto her back, and placed her hand on Angie's face, gently brushing back her hair. "We have a barbecue this afternoon, you know," she whispered.

Angie felt the touch of Kate's hand all the way to her knees, and she parted her lips, letting out a long steady breath of air. The longing in Kate's eyes astonished her. "Can I help?" she whispered back.

Reading ambiguity in the question, and seeing her own want mirrored in Angie's eyes, Angie's mouth grown fuller with desire, Kate moved slightly and kissed Angie on the corner of her mouth. "I don't know," she answered with equal equivocation.

Angie, her arm still around Kate, placed her lips tentatively on Kate's. Kate answered her kiss with equal hesitation, and rested her cheek momentarily on Angie's.

"Angie, sweetheart . . ." Kate whispered her name. She wanted to tell Angie that she loved her. She couldn't bring herself to say the words.

Angie leaned into Kate's ear, nibbled at the lobe. "I want to make love with you. Think about that today while you get things ready for the barbecue, okay?"

Kate swallowed hard. Used to Angie's honesty, why should it unsettle her now? She felt suddenly exposed, embarrassed. Damnit! I'm offering myself to this woman and she's sending me off to think! Once out of her arms, I may never find the courage to come back. "Am I being dismissed?" she asked.

"Oh, Katie . . ." Angie's voice was as ragged as tattered cotton about to come fully unspun. "I don't want to dismiss you. I want to hold you forever." Angie ran her fingertips down Kate's side from her breast to her hip, and in passing felt Kate's pubic hair brush her forearm.

"Well, then . . ." Kate offered.

"Kate, Kate," Angie began. God, she thought, this is delicate. If I could have a hundred women, all I would ever want is Kate. I've been at this long enough to know what I want. But Kate, given her emotional need right now, could find comfort in any woman's arms. She needs healing, and this is where you find it. Maybe all she needs is my warmth. But *I* can't afford to give her that. I'd be selling myself short. Tomorrow she'll be back in Alex's arms, and we'll both pretend this didn't happen, and I'll have to deny what I feel. I can't do it.

"Sweetie, I would never have suspected that you, the impulsive one . . ." *What* was going on in Angie's head? Maybe I'm not desirable.

"Kate!" Angie lifted herself onto one elbow and gave Kate an impish grin. "Will you marry me?"

"What?" Kate laughed in relief. At least it was evident from the question that Angie wasn't rejecting her.

"Katie, I'm not into a one night stand. And I'm not sure where you're at with this. So we make love now, and then what? This afternoon at the barbecue you avert your eyes when I look at you. Next week you transfer me into another department at work. All because you're embarrassed over something that shouldn't have happened. I want you for more than a morning. Your friendship matters to me. I want you to go now, because I want you to come back later, when you've thought about it, and give me what I need — if you can do that. If you don't come back, then we still have our friendship. Understand, sweetheart? I'm not dismissing you. I love you just as much either way."

Kate sighed, playfully wrestled Angie off her elbow, turned her over onto the bed. She felt strong and clean and, yes, the desire was very much there, deep in her groin, overflowing the cup of her heart. Looking down into Angie's startled eyes, she whispered, "You're missing something pretty exciting right now. But you'll be back. And you'll have a hard time getting rid of me."

Strength resided in the possibility of her body as it rested momentarily on Angie's; in the perfection of her power as she surrendered it to another woman. For a fleeting instant she knew that power thus given is power recycled, magnified, returned. Kate held her breath, rested her head on Angie's breast. She felt in her body, within the circle of another's arms, the liberation of a runner for whom time and space explode through infinity, and the spirit surges like a newly created universe. This was freedom. She would be back.

Or maybe she had only been hung over. Kate sipped her wine, and glanced quickly at Angie who sat relaxed on a lawn chair between Alex and Gene Durca. Angie was decked out in all her gold: three neck chains, hoop earrings, bracelet, and two gold rings on the last two fingers of her left hand. Her light beige, sleeveless cotton dress accented her tan.

She's the healthiest woman I've ever seen, Kate told herself. She always looks like an ad for women's sportswear. But now instead of admiring her, I suddenly want to touch. No sooner are my parents gone than I add a whole new problem to my life.

Kate thought back to earlier that afternoon when Alex had arrived. He hadn't been there ten minutes before she had steered him into the bedroom. For the second or third time in their relationship she had allowed him to enter her from above. Normally she could only climax when she straddled him from atop — that position allowed her to feel in control. Because her father had overpowered her —

forced himself on her — she had always, in sexual matters, needed to know that she had the power to direct and lead. Alex had been surprised and pleased by her passion, her surrender to him without foreplay. As usual, she had offered no explanation for her behavior, nor had he asked. She could never have explained that she had been feeling the presence of Angie during the encounter.

What was she going to do with him if she went back to Angie's bed? She was not a Rochelle who could juggle both a man and a woman. Nor, she imagined, would Angie allow that one more time. She would not want Angie to accept it. But what would she tell Alex? As liberal as he was, she couldn't tell him the truth and still face him at the hospital. Angie might be a liberated lesbian — but she herself could *never* see being that way. But was a secret life the kind she wanted to lead? Hadn't that been the way she had always lived — with secrets? Daddy was a secret. There's a syllogism buried somewhere here, her logical mind told her as she sipped her wine.

It was too hot to wear her hair down. Why had she done that? It hung to her mid-back. Alex liked it that way, and although she felt too old for long hair, she was not quite ready to clip her youth. Now she felt foolish. Besides, she hadn't dressed for Alex. She looked down at the light plum color of her dress. A drop of frost had slid off her wine glass and darkened a spot on her lap. It would dry, she reassured herself, hoping Angie hadn't noticed. What was happening here? She was dressing for a woman she had known for five years. A woman! She watched Alex walk to the barbecue. He looked back at her and winked.

"Yeah, I'm dieting too," Kate heard Angie say. Amazed, Kate came out of her private meanderings and looked closely at her friend. Angie caught her eye.

"Hey, Katie, let's get the men a refill." Angie reached for the empty wine glasses, and walked toward the house. Kate followed her into the kitchen.

"You're dieting?" Kate tapped Angie playfully on the shoulder.

Angie removed the wine from the refrigerator, and set it on the counter. She looked at her feet, and then giggled. Her giggling turned into a full laugh, and then tears. Her shoulders shook, and as she tried to gain control of her breathing she said in spurts, "I've . . . never . . . dieted . . . a day . . . in . . . my . . . life!" She held her breath. "Really. I'm stable." Then she started laughing all over again.

Kate threw back her head and laughed too, feeling the tension slide from her body. Angie might worry about her weight — but diet? Never. While Angie had sat there listening so attentively, she must have been in the same mental state that Kate found herself in. Dieting? Angie was in distress, clearly.

"I know, I know." Angie looked chagrined as she faced Kate. "I haven't dieted once in thirty-eight years." Without a pause she switched subjects. "I only wanted to get you in here to tell you how beautiful you look. You know, I've never seen you with your hair down. It's lovely, Kate." Angie touched Kate's hair.

Kate returned her look openly. She wanted to step forward and take Angie in her arms. Instead she replied, "Thank you."

"Are you okay?" Angie asked.

"I'm fine." Kate's green eyes sparkled. "At least I'm enough with the program to realize that instead of dieting, I'm simply not hungry. You're totally out to lunch."

"Thank you, Kate. When you have a deep mind, it can get easily confused on simple issues like that." Angie nodded at her playfully.

"Let's get these glasses outside. If you weren't here, I'd be bored out of my mind," Kate added.

They returned to their lawn chairs. With the men momentarily silent, Angie decided to put her best foot forward. She turned to Gene who was a noted visiting sports podiatrist, and plunged in, "So you've invented a new planter fascitis operation."

"Oh, I didn't realize you're a doctor." The casually dressed man turned with new interest to Angie. "Do you understand about planter fascitis? Of course," he answered himself. "You're a runner! Runners are hypochondriacs. They understand every muscle from the thigh down."

Angie frowned at his patronizing attitude, but at least the annoyance took her mind off Kate. "Inflammation of the longitudinal, ah, heel-to-ball foot arch, right?" She knew damn well she was right because she had memorized the article Kate had given her earlier in the week. "I've never been troubled with it myself . . ." She gave him an equally patronizing smile.

"Right!" Gene smiled pleasantly, and Alex nodded rather proudly.

"Do you actually operate, then?" Like Angie, Kate knew the answer, but she had noticed Angie's frown. Angie might occasionally play the fool but she would never allow herself to be taken for one for too long. Kate felt the need to rescue all of them from a potentially touchy situation.

"Oh, yes." Gene only slowly broke eye contact with Angie.

God, Kate thought, Angie's hooked him. He hasn't the faintest notion that he's insulted her. This ought to be interesting. Would Angie play out her sexual fantasies with Gene, the way she had played hers out with Alex? Were human beings always so transparent? As she turned her attention back to Gene she felt suddenly embarrassed for using Alex that way. "Don't most athletes find surgery a little radical?" she asked.

"That's the beauty of it," Alex piped in with all the joy of a convert. "In the previous procedure you made a large incision on the bottom of the foot — in severe cases of course. But the procedure Gene has developed, well, it's ingenious. You make a tiny incision strategically placed to release part of the facia and alleviate the strain. It's brilliant. So neat!"

"Well, we've had great recovery with it . . ." Gene droned on about conservative therapies, and runners, and this led into a discussion of orthotics.

"You two don't seem to have a very good opinion of runners." Angie looked at both men with a smile. She had had enough of this.

"Well, if you saw as many of them as we do . . ." Gene was unruffled.

"In that case, Kate should just about have her fill of the whole human race. She's seen more of our insides than fish do water."

The men exchanged embarrassed glances, then laughed.

Angie looked at Kate. "I need to let Sophie out. Be back." She got up and retreated as Kate went into an explanation about the new dog.

God, Angie thought. Kate would just have to forgive her. The events of the morning had her rattled. Feet were not the most distracting subject in the world. She couldn't just sit there and look lovingly into Kate's eyes. Christ, would Kate really come back to her? She looked at her manicured fingernails, and considered biting them all off. No, she had worked too hard to break herself of that habit. Maybe the leftover pizza. Before dinner? She wasn't hungry. Oh, God, let her come back.

Chapter 13

Angie placed her suitcase and athletic bag in the closet, walked over to the window. She looked out on the green quad of Squaw Valley, at what had been the 1960 Olympic Village. It was Thursday — less than two weeks from the day Angie referred to privately as "that morning in bed." She and Kate had just arrived for the running clinic.

This was insane, Angie said to herself, so deep in thought she could have been talking out loud. Kate had been wonderful the last twelve days. At work it was Kate who spoke in innuendo, flirted when no one was looking.

Clearly Kate wasn't retreating. But she also wasn't making any direct overtures. Of course, maybe it wasn't something Kate, as a straight woman, had any experience with. Maybe Kate didn't know how to make advances. Well, Angie reminded herself, direct advances weren't her specialty either. Come to think of it, she had been running from Kate ever since that morning. Kate probably thought she was crazy. She was as wound up as a golf ball. Angie sighed and then jumped as she heard Kate enter the room.

"It's warm up here." Kate deposited her luggage. Joining Angie at the window, she studied the sheets of paper in her hand. "Well, there's shoe clinic going on right now," she noted, and placed an arm around Angie's shoulder. "What do you think?"

"Look, Kate!" Angie jumped out from under Kate's arm. "That gray-haired man — the one with the kindly face over there — that's Lyliard!" Angie pointed to a covered patio a hundred yards from their window. Seated around the patio were perhaps thirty runners in various states of attire, most with their shoes off; a middle-aged man stood before them bending a running shoe in his hands. The man Angie had identified sat well outside the circle of runners.

Angie felt relieved with Kate's arm off her shoulder. What *was* she going to do with Kate? Now she was even aware of when Alex spent the night. It cut deep, even though Angie told herself she had no reason to be jealous. Kate had promised her nothing.

Fortunately this confusion and fear, which always came when she fell in love, had only happened twice before — her mercurial personality nearly incinerated when lit by erotic longing. Somehow it seemed more intense this time, maybe because she was trying so hard to

135

hide it from Kate. She didn't want her passion to appear foolish in Kate's eyes. She wanted to reach out with all her strength and pull Kate to her, bury her face in Kate's flesh, taste fully the femininity of her. She was frightened that Kate would flee under such desire. Or worse, find the whole thing disgusting.

"Well, should we go join them?" Kate asked, directing her gaze to the queen-sized bed. Damn her, Kate thought. This woman is as easy to come to as a friend, and impossible to corral as a lover. But Kate had made up her mind with grim, disciplined determination; she was not about to let Angie go. She didn't confront twenty-six miles tentatively or read X rays questioningly. She hadn't been dissuaded by the rigors of medical school nor had she dropped out of track the one time she lost a race. She was not about to turn timid in the face of Angie's fear.

She understood intuitively that Angie was frightened but she didn't understand why. This was a new experience for her — a role reversal. Alex had been the one who never knew her thoughts, who had to dig for explanations that Kate never supplied. Now it was her turn to probe, and she wasn't sure how to go about it.

"I think we should take our shoes off first, don't you? They seem to be heavy into feet out there." God, Angie thought, they had to get out of this room, even if it meant another exploration of feet.

Kate laughed as they headed for the door. "After the podiatry conference comes lunch." Kate turned and raised an eyebrow. "Does that pique your interest?"

"Absolutely. Then what?"

"Frankly, sweetie, I don't think you're ready for the then what."

"Give me a break, Kate. I'm putty in your hands." Angie sighed, avoiding eye contact with Kate.

136

Kate laughed, reassured that they were thinking along the same lines. She looked at the schedule. "Then we get to be filmed running. Then a hike up to some lake . . . hey, look at this! Tomorrow afternoon there's a rafting trip down the Truckee River. Sounds like fun."

The podiatry lecture brought no new knowledge. Debating shoes, a second language to Kate, quickly brought her to the attention of the other runners. Careful not to upstage the podiatrist who led the discussion, she brought up questions he was sure to find challenging but answerable. Someone asked Lyliard about the shoes he was wearing — a new line he had designed. Angie studied the shoes closely, and discovered in the process of a conversation with Lyliard, his old face leathered and his skin sagging with age, that the man was a flirt and great story teller. Before lunch was announced, the night's movie schedule was given. There would be a film on the 1976 Olympic marathon trials, and one on New Zealand long-distance runners.

Lunch was a banquet, bread and all the makings for sandwiches — sliced beef, turkey, salami, swiss and cheddar cheese, crushed avocado, bean sprouts, shredded carrots — together with bowls of fresh fruit, cookies and pies, and a variety of sparkling drinks — all served buffet style. The silent concentration on the faces of the runners indicated how seriously they undertook this part of their training.

Men and women in equal numbers and of all ages sat scattered around picnic tables. Kate and Angie joined a table, and began the pleasant exchange of running histories — When and why did you first start running?

What was the toughest run you ever did? — stories that allow runners an immediate, easy familiarity.

An afternoon hike began under a stark clean sky, on a path that snaked vertically through pine trees and loose dirt, then opened out on a hill of late blooming lilies and boulders the size of small houses. At a fast clip the hikers breathlessly followed the spray of a downward cascading stream. Kate kept pace with Jeff Galloway. Olympian-turned-entrepreneur, he impressed her with his knowledge and seriousness. She would submit her running schedule and goals to him and Lyliard. Saturday morning they would hold a conference with her.

By dinnertime both women felt as though they had been there all week. The company of like-minded runners, free of large egos, gravitated toward a conviviality that wisely accepted differences of opinions while poking around gently for commonality. Kate felt her hospital tensions slide away. Angie followed Lyliard around like a puppy, delightedly taking in his every story. During dinner Angie and Kate looked at each other, both of their dark faces freshly brushed a sunburnt red, and the personal strain they had known for two weeks dissolved in a wash of accord.

Kate, hearing the shower running as she came into the room, saw this as an opportunity. Angie couldn't run away from her in the shower. "Can I shower with you?" She poked her head into the bathroom. Suddenly she was frightened that Angie might say no. Or saying yes, Angie might not like her body. Had Angie ever *really* looked at her before? Oh sure, they had sat in the steam room together at the health club. But maybe Angie was only being polite when she had commented on her body. Surely

Angie hadn't looked at her as a woman with whom she would be making love. Angie hadn't seen the slight sag in her skin or the inevitable thickening of age.

Angie's stomach flipped as though she had descended eighty floors on a broken elevator. She peered around the shower curtain at Kate who stood a little within the bathroom, waiting for a response. "Katie . . ." She took a deep breath. "You're driving me crazy. Come in here."

As she watched Kate undress, removing the running shorts and singlet she had worn all day, a calm settled over Angie. Kate, when she stepped into the shower, would enter her world — the lesbian circle of rapture given, delight taken. Angie reminded herself that all she had to do, all she could do, was be true to her love of women, and the rest would take care of itself. This immediate moment was a simple voyage into another woman's pleasure, a sharing of her own. The time for thought was over. Now was a time of discovery.

Kate stepped into the shower, and stared at Angie's back, as Angie, standing under the shower head, finished lathering the front of her body. Kate felt as though she were looking at Angie for the first time, and she slowly savored the view of her — the full muscles in her shoulders glistening with splashes of water, her small waist curving gracefully in before sweeping down into hips and a fully rounded ass that with only a few demarcations passed down into the long smooth hamstrings of Angie's upper legs. Aware that she had never looked at another woman this way — admired perhaps, but never absorbed the curve of feminine lines — Kate drank the moment before her, and realized, even as a languorous weakness swept her, that Angie, no child, no novice, was offering her this view as a gift both complete in itself and as prologue. There was no awkwardness, no self-consciousness in her motion as Angie turned, nipples erect, her large gray eyes attentive, and faced her.

Angie understood immediately that Kate was emotionally strong and unafraid. She allowed her eyes to slowly wander down Kate's body, caressing her in deep visual drafts. How many times had she looked at this body, allowed herself to only half-see it? Now she could look free of all restraint. Seeing the spread of Kate's shoulders, the easy fullness of Kate's breasts, the flatness of the abdomen, the blonde pubic hair, Angie marveled, and was pleased that Kate did not become coy under such scrutiny. She wanted to exchange bodies with Kate, feel Kate's skin wrap around her, covering her, feel her heart dissolve in Kate's liquid fullness. Her eyes came back to Kate's. "You must be cold." There was no need to tell Kate how beautiful she was; Angie felt herself pour into the small space between them the totality of her meaning without any need for words. "Here, get under the water."

Kate didn't move. She had seen her own beauty in Angie's eyes. Yes, she had been desired before, but no eyes had so openly praised, so eloquently addressed her. Without moving, Angie had yielded before her. Yet if Angie stood before her as weak in surrender as Kate felt, then who was in control? Shock tapped at Kate's mind. This was a dance where no one led. They would create together what neither could sustain alone — the heat that fanned the core fire of existence. At forty-two Kate suddenly knew this was a discovery all lovers made anew.

"Angie," Kate whispered. "You have the soap. Wash me." Kate brushed past Angie, moved underneath the water, her back to Angie.

But Angie turned Kate around; slowly began to lather her. The smoothness of soap intensified Kate's softness, but also made the solidity of touch illusive, heightening

Angie's craving. Kate's breasts slid gently within her palms. Angie's lips parted, and her hands quivered as she moved the soap down Kate's stomach. Kate closed her eyes and tilted her head back as Angie moved the soap between her legs, legs that she spread for Angie's access. Angie's breath quickened in response, her stomach moved. Caressing the inside of Kate's thighs, she rubbed her hands slowly up and down.

Kate swayed slightly in her hands. Angie moved into her, resting Kate against her body. Kate placed her face in Angie's neck and made an inarticulate sound. Her arms around Kate, applying light pressure with the palms of both hands, Angie pressed Kate into her hips, undulating upward, searching for the softness under Kate's pelvic bone. Moving one arm up, she folded Kate into her own small breasts, and felt, from her cheek to her knees, the full blending of Kate's body with hers.

"Katie, I can't stand up another moment." Angie, her voice husky, moved Kate back a step, and without looking at her, splashed water over her soapy body. "Come to bed with me."

Kate smiled and weakly flicked water back into Angie's face.

Even though Kate thought she remembered perfectly the kiss of two weeks before, the softness of Angie's mouth surprised her. Angie's cheek felt like the fuzzy surface of an African violet. The malleable tenuousness of Angie's tongue nibbling at the corners of her mouth suddenly shocked her. Is this what a woman feels like to a man — a pliable surface that recedes with each advance? How maddening. How exciting.

Angie's breath warmed her ear. She guided Angie's throat to her mouth, and smelled the clear richness of her fragrance. Moving Angie's face to her own searching lips, she closed her eyes completely, and flowed effortlessly upon a current of delicate affection. Kate opened her mouth and made a passage through which Angie entered her.

She felt Kate under her like a cashmere sky spread to eternity. She reclined there, prevailing like a breeze, touching with her hands pleasures hidden in recess from the mind.

She penetrated her fluid grace; felt Kate's moisture surround her fingers. She felt the contractions inside herself, as she felt Kate contract around her. Kate grew larger beneath her strokes; taut, Angie went with her breath for breath, moaning delight at each peak of ascension, her heart a mirror of Kate's journey.

Satisfaction came only to elevate each into newer levels of desire, into a surfeit of pleasure breathtaking in its ancient novelty and splendor.

"You," Kate whispered into Angie's stomach, "are life after death."

"Heaven can only be had on earth when it's had with another . . . with you," Angie whispered into Kate's hair.

Chapter 14

With Kate beside her quietly reading the Sunday paper, Angie surveyed the Sacramento skyline as she drove. She loved Sacramento with all its trees — more per capita, she knew, than any other city in the world. In fact, there were very few skyscrapers — the state capitol dome had always been visible when driving in from San Francisco until recently; several new developments now obscured it. Oh sure, Sacramento was not cosmopolitan. But compared to the Mendocino coast where she had grown up, it was a metropolis. San Francisco, to which she drove at least once a week, was only a hundred miles away and had all the cultural diversity Sacramento lacked. Of course, Sacramento made up for its cultural deficiencies with historical significance. Sutter's Fort, in mid-town, surrounded by high palms, oaks and pines, stepped right out of the 19th Century, and was surrounded by all the Victorian homes Angie loved. Maybe someday she and Kate would have one . . .

Angie drove the Porsche up onto the freeway, and noted with deep contentment the change of seasons. October was her favorite month: harvest time, when all the trees were drunk with color. Pumpkins as big as the moon, and pomegranates, persimmons, and early citrus began showing up in the farmers' markets around town. The startling blue skies and flaming vegetation reminded her of a medieval faire. Angie's whole sense of history came together in this month which ran before the upcoming holidays like a herald trumpeting a royal birth or wedding, when nature herself threw a festive dance for her children.

Shifting into fourth gear, Angie took her eyes off the road and said, "You radiate when you smile. I can't get enough of you."

She wondered, an edge of anxiety coming into this perfect morning, if Kate would really stay with her. Then she reminded herself that it didn't matter. If some disaster happened tomorrow and she were never to see Kate again, then the last month would be enough to sustain her forever. Kate had shared with her a pleasure and a peace and a confidence in living which though always a part of her that Angie had admired, came through even more solidly when Kate was in love. Angie did not doubt that Kate was in love with her.

"You make me radiate, sweetie." Kate squeezed Angie's hand and returned her gaze to the comics. "Do

144

you know, Mark Twain once said that comedy keeps the heart sweet?"

"We're doing a comedy here?" Angie questioned and then laughed.

"Isn't that what it feels like?" Kate countered. "I feel like laughing all the time. I smile most of the time."

"Romeo and Juliet was a tragedy," Angie reminded her.

"Ah, proving only that the young take these things much too seriously." The tan lines at the corners of Kate's eyes creased.

"I love you!" Angie exploded and rumpled Kate's hair.

Kate squeezed Angie's hand and placed it on her thigh. She rested her head against the seat rest, closed her eyes. "God, I feel wonderful!" she whispered, not yet ready to tell Angie she loved her — the words didn't begin to convey what she felt.

Funny, she thought, how untroubled she was by her relationship with Angie. Oh, she wasn't ready to announce it to the world, but if the world found out, she would defend the relationship with her dying breath. That's a little dramatic, she smiled to herself. Something Angie might say. Kate felt proud of her relationship with Angie, and her only hesitation was not out of shame, but out of all the unloving ways the world could find to demean that relationship.

Still . . . maybe it was her age. At forty-two you knew yourself a little better than you did at twenty. Or knowing yourself less well, accepted with humor those things you did not understand. For the first time in her life, Kate felt full and complete in her body. Her running even felt better — as if it were an extension of her health rather than an obsession to gain control of her life. Angie's touch was a healing miracle; Angie's wholeness and enthusiasm like a radical implantation that imparted life. Angie made her feel like the most special person God had placed on earth, and when she felt Angie melt under her touch all notions of power became obsolete. This wasn't just love — this was the secret of the universe, the wonder that keeps the stars apart. What had e. e. cummings said? *Whatever a sun will always sing is you.* Kate opened her eyes and, looking at Angie, was silently amazed to see once again the missing piece of her own internal puzzle.

Angie interrupted her thoughts. "Not upset over Alex leaving?"

She still couldn't believe that Kate could let go of Alex so easily — that she had let go of him at all. She was equally surprised that he hadn't put up more of a fight. That Kate was so confident, so sure in her decision, was something Angie didn't want to question for fear everything would fall apart. At the same time, she didn't want any unresolved doubts festering in Kate's mind, to later infect and destroy their happiness. What she really wanted to tell Kate was that she was willing to grieve the loss of Alex with her — this was not something to be forgotten in the euphoria of love. But to say that sounded too patronizing.

"Strange how things work out . . . almost magically," Kate replied.

Alex had come over to the house as excited as a little boy who had won all the marbles in the schoolyard. He insisted they go out to Bon Appetit for dinner — one of the most expensive restaurants in town. Kate, on the other hand, had chosen this night to break things off with him. It was painful from the beginning; only easier because of what he had to say.

"Gene has an opening for me — for me, Kate!" He clinked his glass of costly chardonnay against hers. "This is what I've wanted for the last three years. Think of it! I even love Seattle." He drank expansively.

"You're moving to Seattle?" Kate was surprised.

"What do you mean?" He looked at her perplexed. "We're getting married and moving there *together*. This has been a wonderful affair — but it's time to move on into the world of married bliss, don't you think?" He laughed.

"Alex." She put down her wine and looked at him seriously. "It *has* been a wonderful affair. But I'm not moving to Seattle." She debated whether to tell him that regardless of Seattle, the affair was over. She waited to see his reaction. She might not have to tell him.

"Katie, this is an opportunity of a lifetime. I can't pass it up —"

She leaned over the table toward him and took his hands. "You shouldn't. You should go. Really, Alex. It's just that I won't go with you."

"Kate! Don't say that!" He looked down at her hands, looked up at her, confusion in his eyes.

"Yes." Kate nodded. She tightened her grip. "Without me." She watched him weigh his ambition and his love, his anger and his need.

"We're over?" He shook his hands free. "This means we're through? Kate, please tell me you'll at least think about it. I told him I'd be up in a month." His voice was pleading. Tears filled his eyes.

"Alex, I love you. And there is nothing to think about. You'll find another nice woman in Seattle. You deserve the very best."

"I don't understand . . ."

No, he hadn't understood. They had left the restaurant without eating, Alex stonily silent. He had called several times — pleading and angry, had made one last phone call from the airport. Kate cried over the loss of him, over her relief, over her own inability to have loved him better.

Angie parked the car. She and Kate followed other runners to a clearing where a banner proclaimed: BADGER HILL FIVE MILE RUN. Perhaps three hundred runners in various attire, from full warmup suits to brief shorts and singlets, milled around the clearing; some stood half asleep in the registration and pre-registration lines; others danced impatiently around portable restrooms; still others distorted their bodies in a variety of yoga postures, stretching the sleep out of their muscles. A picnic table held huge containers of water. Benches groaned with unopened gallons of apple juice.

Angie sighed deeply, and suddenly wondered why she was here. In the flush of her emotional attachment to Kate, had she actually decided to commit herself to a foot race? This had to be love. But she was nervous and excited, and love almost seemed like a poor excuse right now. Maybe it had been the running camp and associating with all those runners which made this madness seem normal. No, it was Kate. Running was a bond between them, and now her commitment to racing and to this race was an extension of her commitment to Kate as a lover. She sighed again.

Kate took her to a registration table. They were given racing numbers and safety-pins to attach the numbers to their shirts. Angie eyed the boxes of green T-shirts behind the table. Walking to the table, she asked one of the assistants if she could see one. The assistant smiled and held up a T-shirt emblazoned with the name of the race, the distance to be run, and the sponsoring Sierra Club logo. The Sierra Club had a nice logo, and Angie decided the shirt was quite handsome. Green wasn't her color, and she would never wear it with her wool winter pants, but then . . . she just simply had to have this shirt. She thanked the assistant and walked over to Kate who was stretching against a tree.

"Chic?" Kate raised a teasing eyebrow.

"What?" Angie had no idea what Kate was talking about.

"The T-shirt, sweetie. Your prize. You can wear it when you take me out dancing." Kate lowered her voice with the last comment.

"But listen." Angie's voice held alarm. "What if I'm the last one in and all the shirts are gone. What then?"

"Unless you fall and break a leg, honey, I promise you will not be the last one in."

"Good reason to run as fast as you can." A slender man had been eavesdropping, eyeing Angie appreciatively.

"Kate, can I have yours if I'm the last one in and they run out?" Angie ignored the man, not out of meanness but out of panic that she might not get a shirt.

The man looked at Kate and smiled. "The woman has no shame."

"None," Kate assured him and smiled back.

"Five minutes to race time," a voice yelled over the crowd.

"Or what if they don't have the right size?" Ever fashion-conscious, Angie was gripped by a new anxiety even as Kate led her over to the starting line.

"Okay, Angie," Kate said, ignoring this latest concern. "We position ourselves according to our pace.

The ten minute milers start in the back, the five minute milers in front. How fast do you want to run?"

"Kate." Angie had a compulsive look in her eyes. "What if I run two miles out and turn around and run back in? It wouldn't be five miles, I know. But I'd get a T-shirt."

"Angelina, I'm shocked!" Kate gently batted the side of Angie's head. "Runners never cheat. We are an honorable group, child."

"*Mi scusi.*" Reprimanded like a child, Angie lapsed into the Italian reply she used to give her mother and looked at her feet. "I lost my head. Must be the tension." The adult in her quickly returned. "How fast are you going to run?"

Kate looked at Angie and shook her head. It hadn't occurred to her that Angie would be nervous. Did Angie have a competitive side she wasn't aware of? "I think I'll go for six minute miles. That sounds sensible, doesn't it? But there are hills so —"

"Hills!" Angie screamed. "Mother of God, Kate, I don't *do* hills. I'll never get a T-shirt."

The starting gun went off. With all their talking, Kate had missed the pre-race information given by the race director about what to expect on the course, where the timers would be, the water stops. Because she didn't know where the hills were, she didn't know how to pace herself. She hadn't noticed too many people in her age group, but that was always hard to judge. The desire to go out fast and win a medal welled up inside but looking at Angie, she resisted. She would stay with Angie for the first mile. Maybe for the entire race, she told herself. Angie needed her.

The first two hundred feet were level, the next slightly up. Then came a mile of nearly vertical downhill. Both women were silent, picking their way carefully around rocks, dry crenelated dirt, the narrow trail itself.

"Kate, Kate." Angie was slightly breathless, but considering her pace and the fact that she was keeping up with Kate, she was doing fine. "What goes down, must come up?"

"You're reading my mind," Kate admitted. Was Angie going to kill herself for a T-shirt? No, she would not allow Angie to continue this pace. "Yes. We have to run back up this. You're doing just great, though. How do you feel?"

"Ecstatic. Assuming death is four miles ahead, this moment is exquisite."

"Poetic." Kate wanted to laugh. "Save your humor for the end, sweetie."

They rounded a bend and for a hundred yards ran parallel to a cow pasture. They could see a woman at the end of the pasture calling out times. Angie and Kate raced by in full stride, both quickening their pace just slightly in order to hear the time sooner.

"Five-fifty-one," the woman called out.

"Oh, my God," Angie panted.

"Don't panic, Angie. It was all downhill. That won't hurt you later. You're fine."

"Okay." Angie rested slightly in her head. "I'm going to have to slow down."

"I'll stay with you." Kate slowed the pace as they came to a slight incline.

"Kate, no." Angie couldn't afford the energy of putting much emotion into her voice, so she chose her words carefully. "You must go ahead. It's up to you to do your best. For both of us. I'll do my best too . . . for both of us. But our bests are not the same. Go ahead."

Kate thought for a moment. It struck her that if she were to stay with Angie, Angie would only struggle to keep up the pace. "Okay. For you, sweetie. And for both our bests."

Kate pulled away slowly. Angie followed her with her eyes. God, the woman looked good from behind. Kate disappeared around a bend, and Angie was left to concentrate on her own effort. She settled into a comfortable pace that varied little despite the rolling hills. In the next mile several runners, mostly men, passed her. The narrow dusty trail broadened into a damp dirt road lined with pine trees.

At the two mile mark a long-haired teen-age boy announced her time: 13:21. That was still pretty good, she assured herself as the trail took a sharp turn to the left, narrowed, became a sweeping stream of gullies that Angie followed with her head down because she didn't want to get her feet wet. Without warning — because she wasn't looking up — the path headed straight uphill. Pine trees provided shade and creeping vegetation held in moisture. A stream sounded along the trail, overgrowth preventing all but an occasional glimpse of it.

Her breathing became labored. Angie decided to enjoy the environment, even as her pace slackened. Up the trail she noticed a woman in red shorts. At the same time she glimpsed what had to be the front runner coming down the mountain. He leaped the gullies, bounding in perfect concentration from foot to foot, and Angie saw as he passed how drenched with sweat he was. She gave him a tiny cheer through her own painful panting.

The uphill went on and on. Angie's thighs were a heavy ache. Her mind talked to her about walking. Okay, at the next turn we'll walk, she addressed her mind as though it were a separate being.

She could still make out the woman in red ahead of her; the woman seemed to be slowing. Maybe, just maybe,

I can catch her, Angie thought excitedly, forgetting she had decided to walk.

More runners came down the hill, some in groups. The stream and the environment faded in Angie's mind, and she looked hopefully at the returning runners for inspiration and comfort. She saw the first woman runner, and smiled weakly at her; the woman was too lost in concentration to notice. More runners. Two more women. Angie counted the women, thinking she would be able to judge Kate's place. Finally she saw Kate's yellow and black striped shorts, and with renewed energy raised her hand.

"Three women ahead of you!" She shouted at Kate.

"Thanks. You're looking good," Kate called back in encouragement. "Keep it up."

Then Kate was gone, and once again, only with more finality, Angie was left to her own thoughts. The thoughts became less and less coherent. All that mattered was making it to the turn-around point and the water. It was all uphill, Angie marveled, too tired to rage.

She rounded a corner, and saw the water stop. She smiled insanely at the woman who handed her some ice water, and she stopped.

"Keep running," a man in a striped shirt yelled at her in a kindly way. "Now's no time to stop."

"In a minute." Angie gagged on the water.

"Come on!" yelled an old man by the water table. He didn't appear to be yelling at her and she turned around to see a man and a woman run up to the table, each taking a cup while continuing to jog past her. Angie threw her cup down amid all the others littering the area, and took off.

A blond man called out her three mile time: 22:13. That was all right, she assured herself. At least now she could make up maybe thirty seconds on the downhill. In a silent swoop she passed the man and woman who had overtaken her at the water stop.

Slowly she calculated her time. The first mile in nearly six minutes, the second in seven, the third in eight. Didn't look too good — still, if she could do this one in seven, it would be fine. She caught sight of the woman in the red shorts again. Ah, ha. She *would* pass her. And she did.

At the bottom of the mountain she slowed slightly and caught her breath. Now the rolling hills. She heard her four mile time and smiled grimly. Twenty-nine thirteen. Good. She had made her seven minute mile. *Marvelioso,* she heard her mother say.

She lost all sense of time and place, determined only to do the best she could. Tomorrow she would sleep late, she promised herself again and again. Maybe she wouldn't run for a day or two. Maybe she would be sore for a week. Mountains. She wasn't trained for mountains, dammit. Mexican food. She'd take Kate out for Mexican food . . .''

She started up the final hill, and suddenly remembered that this was the beginning of the end — the final mile. No one was around. The cow pasture stretched out briefly. She heard someone behind. But then, she reminded herself proudly, she had passed a great many runners. Some had been walking. There had been a large number of women still going uphill to the water as she had come down. She *would* get a T-shirt. Size didn't matter. Maybe she would frame it on the wall. She laughed at herself. Who cares? Who really cares?

She pushed on. Elation gripped her. She was a runner now. Like Kate. A real runner. She was ahead of lots of people. The pain in her legs felt nearly friendly, a reminder of her strength.

The elation vanished. Her mind once again babbled about walking, telling her she had done better than good. Each step became a raging battle with gravity. Sweat dripped in a drizzling rain from her upper body and face. She decided in the future she would run only three mile races . . . on flat surfaces. Her pace slowed, then slowed even more, but she would not walk. Coming onto the rise that led mostly downhill to the finish, she only imitated a run; her pace was slower than a medium walk.

Yet coming over the rise, and seeing the finish line, she picked herself up with all her pride and kicked out for the finish. She crossed and heard her time as if from an enormous distance: 38:12.

A woman in the finish chute gave her a cup of water, took her number with her age and name from her wet shirt, gave her a ticket for a T-shirt, and told her where to go for the apple juice.

Kate grabbed Angie the moment she left the chute, embraced her.

"Look at you! I thought you'd be another five minutes. You have great speed, sweetie. Great! And guts. There's a racer inside you!" Pride filled Kate's excited voice.

Angie looked at Kate. She could not speak and wanted to cry. She felt like neither a winner nor a loser. She stood momentarily outside of time and all its categories — transcendently present. It was more triumph than her heart could hold.

The moment broke, and Angie grabbed Kate. "How did you do? Did you win?"

"A piece of cake." Kate raised an arm as she led Angie to the T-shirts. "How do *you* feel?" Kate ruffled Angie's wet head.

"Kate," Angie's voice broke with emotion and tears came to her eyes, "I can't believe that people come out here and call out times, and mark trails, and pass out water — just so we can feel like this. I'm so touched," she sniffled.

"Ah." Kate's green eyes broadened into a smile that slipped around Angie as cleanly as satin.

The One Who Directs had brought him here. A cottage. Confusion touched him. Could the One Who Directs ever be wrong? He forgot the thought; his thinking mind numbed over as though of ice encapsulated.

Execute, the One Who Directs had said. At first he had not understood. His lightning was for shock. Electrocute, the One Who Directs had said. Then he had understood. The Son of Thunder will not be denied. The power of life and death were his. The Shewitches must be no more; they had laughed at his lightning, they had mocked divine retribution. Jezebels slithered across the land. Delilahs conspired with the enemy and robbed manhood of its rightful place. He must electrocute the Shewitches and their daughters. The time of grace was over.

So tired. Had a Shewitch drugged him? They had offered him strong drink. He had refused. They ran their fingers down him and laughed. As he sat in the bar, surrounded by evil, the One Who Directs whispered in his ear, Do you understand now? Yes, he understood. The Son of Thunder could not sleep.

He lowered his mask, and tried the window. Open. The Shewitch would not be home. He knew where she was. He knew everything with clarity.

The stench of a thousand Shewitches flung up and invaded his limbs as he entered. The holiness of his mission pushed back the invasion. Potency reclaimed it rightful dominion, mightiness rippled in his scepter. The One Who Directs was near, commanding strength throughout his imperium. Now was the glory. Now the tiredness dissolved as he rose up to meet the Director.

He walked to the silkscreen and slashed it asunder with one full swipe of his hand. He flung the azalea to the floor. His ecstasy soared with the crash of porcelain.

In the distance his perfect hearing picked up the whining bark of a small dog. He laughed.

Chapter 15

Kate sat bolt upright in bed, then realized that the noise she had heard was only Sophie scratching at the bedroom door to get out. "Sophie, come here," Kate whispered. The little dog scampered over to her. "Sophie, let this not become a habit," she muttered as she carried the puppy to the door. "I know your mother is more than pleased that you now know how to ask to be let out. But the middle of the night is not *when* you should ask."

Angie rolled over and reached for Kate as she slipped back into bed. Kate felt cold, and Angie wrapped her arms around her. "Thank you for letting her out."

"Um." Kate drew Angie's mouth to hers. She still couldn't touch Angie enough, and it had been two months. At work she caressed her with her eyes, careful not to touch her physically. Once she had touched this woman so thoughtlessly; it hadn't mattered who saw because it meant nothing more than friendship. Now she couldn't be casual even when looking at her. God, Kate thought, I feel ten years younger; how could everyone not know? People were actually commenting on how good she looked lately. She wanted to shout to the world that she was in love. This was the fountain of youth Ponce de Leon sought — the water that rinses away accumulations of disappointment and restores the confidence of youth.

"Nice," Angie murmured against her ear. "You're so incredibly loving. God, you feel good." Angie stroked Kate's shoulder and ran her fingernails down her back.

Outside Sophie barked. Both women groaned, neither wanting to get up. "Kids," Angie grumbled.

"She sounds a little frantic." Kate sat up and listened.

"You're right." Angie jumped out of bed and threw on a sweatshirt. "She's not at the door."

Angie stepped outside, her teeth instantly chattering in the cold November air. The valley was trapped in a thick white mist known to local residents as the tule fog. The moon filtered slightly through it, casting trees, fences, neighboring structures in dull moist silhouettes. Angie shuddered and looked for Sophie, spotted her over at the cottage scratching underneath a window.

"Sophie, come."

Angie raised her voice, but the dog adamantly scratched under the window. Angie cursed. She walked across the backyard, the prickly grass wet and cold beneath her bare feet.

160

"Sophie, no." She picked up the dog. "You'll wake the whole neighborhood."

Then she noticed that the window was open. She frowned. Although she still worked in the cottage, using it as a study, she never opened the window — certainly not at this time of year. Could Kate have opened it?

Sophie in her arms, she turned to go back: then turned again and looked into the window. In the moon shadows, the place looked turned upside down. Sophie barked again, wriggled in Angie's arms, trying to get into the cottage. The front door broke open. A figure in a ski mask darted out, ran for the back fence. Without a second's hesitation Angie released Sophie, ran for the house and Kate.

Sprinting into the bedroom, Angie shouted, "Kate, the rapist!"

Angie had her running shorts on in seconds. Kate leaped from the bed as Angie raced out the back door.

Kate asked herself as she fought her way into a T-shirt and her shorts why she had not held Angie back. Surely the rapist was no danger to them — was probably already over the fence. But Angie had flown out of the house with all the impetuous certainty of her nature. Kate was out the back door only seconds behind her.

Angie dashed for the fence, and leaped. Poised at the top, she quickly looked around, then dropped onto the ground. The distant fleeing form was profiled in the shimmering moonlight, running across a vacant field, certain of his destination, heading for the bike trail. Angie increased her pace. Behind her, she heard Kate hit the ground as she jumped off the fence.

Angie ran in headlong pursuit. I'll get the son-of-a-bitch, she raged. He was in *my* cottage! He was after me! Now he'll know what it's like — having someone after him. Anger pounded in her mind, and her legs responded with a powerful surging.

Thorny weeds ripped at her ankles, pebbles punctured her feet. Her concentration, complete as a circle, blocked out all pain. Sweat started down her forehead. She saw only the form before her. She felt she was gaining. The form turned away from the field and onto the street. He turned left at the next corner. That street, she knew, deadended at the levee. She rounded the corner, sprinted up the incline to the levee as the form disappeared down the other side.

Kate drew even with her at the top of the levee. Without speaking or stopping, they surveyed the land. As they raced down the other side, a figure turned onto the bike trail and disappeared into the shrubs, the trees, the foggy night.

Kate bolted onward, reaching the bike trail a dozen feet ahead of Angie. The trail zig-zagged, she couldn't see clearly. She began to calculate: They must have been running close to a 5:30 pace for a good mile. The man had to be in good shape, probably young, maybe a seasoned runner. But if he wasn't a runner, even allowing for adrenalin, he couldn't keep this up. He might very well be a conditioned athlete — newspaper accounts had suggested that the rapist was a biker. But even a biker couldn't keep up this pace running.

A half mile down the trail consciousness slowly intruded. This was not a race, for God's sake. What was she doing figuring pace when she and Angie were in terrible danger? What would they do if they caught him? Panting, she slowed, stopped. In seconds Angie was beside her.

"What's the matter?" Angie was bent double, trying to catch her breath.

162

"The matter?" Kate hadn't caught her breath either. "The matter?" she repeated, as though the question were answer enough.

"Right." Angie instantly understood. "Let's get the hell out of here." This was crazy. She was not about to further endanger either of them with this foolishness. She wanted a long life with Kate. Chasing a rapist in the middle of the night — insane!

Slowly they trotted back. They began to breathe normally. Furtively they glanced around, checking trees and shrubs and high grass for signs of a shadow or moving figure. Near the last tree, close to the lane leading back up to the levee, Angie grabbed Kate's arm and stopped.

Angie looked slowly to her left, then to her right. She felt her mind and body lock in tension. "Listen."

The river with a slow steady surge rustled softly along its banks. The rest was silence, wrapped loosely in the muted fog. Angie felt fear assault her sweating body like a spear of ice. She and Kate were not alone, and she knew it.

Kate took Angie by the shoulder and pushed her gently forward. She spoke slowly, in a low voice. "Listen, carefully. He sees us. That's okay. We can run faster. Don't panic. He simply has to be exhausted. He won't catch us. He won't even try. Run, honey." Kate picked up the pace as she spoke. "Just a little faster. Back to the house. It's okay."

Up the levee they raced, gravel puncturing their feet. Back across the field behind the house. Kate kept up a monologue of encouragement for Angie; alert yet calming, void of panic, Kate led her with her voice as a seeing eye leads the blind. Jumping back over the fence, Angie slumped against it. Sophie leaped excitedly at her legs.

Kate folded Angie into her arms. "Let's go into the cottage," she directed. They needed to engage in some kind of activity, Kate reasoned. To clean their wounds, and reclaim their territory. Now, together.

* * * * *

COWARD!

No. He shook his head. No, he was not a coward.

Yes, the One Who Directs taunted back. I give you an order, and you run like a scared girl. You do not deserve to be the Son of Thunder. I will find another.

I am the Son of Thunder, he replied.

Then you must go back, and rid the realm of these Shewitches. They are an abomination to me.

He rose from the tall grass. In the distance he saw the Shewitches disappear over the levee.

Exhaustion. Tired. He placed one foot in front of the other. The One Who Directs talked incessantly; the voice held him firmly in a steel grip, pushing each heavy leg onward.

Even as he pushed on, a fire rampaged his brain, melting in small drops the ice that held him captive. He leaped for the fence, feeling the drops of sweat fall from his body. He felt as if he were made of candle-wax and each drop of sweat were a segment of skin peeled slowly away.

He stood on the cold wet grass, sinew and bare veins and nerve endings exposed to the air, shadows licking at the raw underside of his dissolving parts.

DIE, the voice ordered.

The gray moist night faded into black. Nothing but black and then nothing at all.

The voice stood alone and smiled. The Son of Thunder was dead. The One Who Directs now had a body of its own — a mind to perfect its mission.

It walked to the cottage and blew open the door with one all-powerful movement.

Chapter 16

Angie and Kate whirled to face the direction of exploding sound. The figure filled the door frame and paused there, high-pitched laughter gushing from its mouth and filling the room. Sophie barked.

Both women stood frozen in the middle of the living room, facing the man in the door. Then Kate quickly pushed Angie toward the bedroom, dividing the intruder's attention. Turning back, she shoved the couch toward him, forcing him to deal with her.

"I have you now," a high-pitched voice addressed her. A series of surreal giggles flowed through the small round opening in his ski mask. He took a step into the cottage, threw wide his arms. "I have you."

Kate looked around the room, her gaze brushing the floor in front of her. The gun. She saw Angie's gun. It must have been under the couch. She swooped down with one movement and came up with the weapon, slapping it into her left hand, bracing it firmly in both hands, pointing it directly at the intruder.

"A mere toy," the intruder chortled in falsetto. He took another step toward her.

"One more step and I'll shoot you," Kate warned in a steady voice, praying silently that the safety wasn't on. "You can turn around and leave, but one more step and I shoot." She bent her knees — the way she had seen hundreds of detectives do in movies — and braced for the impact of firing.

The intruder paused for a moment and then took another step forward. "You're not going to shoot," the voice trilled.

Kate aimed the gun at the man's legs. She pulled the trigger. Her eyes slammed shut as her arms flexed upward. The deafening explosion of the .38 made her ears ring. The intruder seemed to take another step toward her, and she fired again, this time at his mid-section. He lurched drunkenly toward the couch, his head jerked up and then fell as his whole body slumped forward. Blood sputtered from the mouth-opening in his ski mask. His chin caught the back of the couch. He landed on his back between the door and the back of the couch.

Kate bolted toward him, gun still in one hand, as Angie ran toward her. "No," Kate commanded, and held Angie back with an outstretched arm as she appraised the figure on the floor.

167

"Take this." Kate handed the gun to Angie. "And call an ambulance. I'll be right back."

As Kate raced out the door, Angie held the gun and stared at the figure on the floor. An ambulance, she heard Kate's voice echo in her ear. An ambulance? Backing into the kitchen, keeping the man on the floor covered with the gun, she reached for the phone and with one hand dialed the nine-one-one emergency number.

Immediately a woman's voice came on the line. Angie, startled by the sound of her own voice told the woman that "we" had just shot a man who was now bleeding on the living room floor. "We" needed an ambulance. In a soothing voice, the woman asked questions, and without reflection Angie answered, aware of neither the questions nor her answers.

Even as Angie mechanically talked with the voice on the phone, Kate raced back into the cottage with her black doctor's bag, and knelt before the bleeding form. Wanting to immediately examine any head injury, she carefully rolled back the ski mask, opening her bag at the same time.

"My God!" Angie gasped. *"It's Scott!"*

The telephone receiver fell from her hand.

Kate looked up and calculated Angie's physical and emotional condition, her hands never once forgetting to continue clearing the blood from Scott's face, probing for the bullet's point of entry, noting his vital signs. The wound in Scott's leg did not concern her.

"Boil water, sweetie," Kate addressed Angie in a gentle voice while checking Scott's eyes and feeling the back of his head.

"Okay." Angie rushed into the kitchen. Water flowed. Pans clanked.

168

Kate heard what she assumed to be blood gurgling in Scott's throat even as his breathing grew increasingly erratic. Kate pushed back the thought that he was struggling — the man before her lay unconscious — as she opened his mouth, feeling inside with her fingers. That was it! The bullet had entered his mouth, split his tongue, and was now swelling the muscle in his throat, blocking his breathing. He could go into respiratory arrest at any moment. As sirens sounded in the late night, she grabbed a scalpel from her bag, and made a small incision at the base of Scott's neck.

Angie darted out the door, presumably to direct the emergency personnel to the cottage. Kate was relieved that Angie now had something concrete to do.

She continued working, placing a c-shape tube in the incision, seeing Scott's rapid respiration stabilize. He could now breathe and her own breathing eased with his. She hoped he had not gotten blood in his lungs but there was nothing she could do if he had. She stuffed his mouth with gauze, attempting to stop or at least contain the bleeding. She swiftly applied a pressure dressing to the bullet hole in his leg. Examining his reflexes, she determined that there was probably no damage to his spinal cord. She looked at him, searching for something else to be done.

Her doctor's mind said she had done all she could. She looked at him again, slowly. Her heart broke.

When Angie and the paramedics and the sheriffs entered, Kate was still bent over Scott, caressing his damp head with her damp cheek, whispering in his ear, tending to him not as a doctor, but as a sister does a fallen brother — in disbelieving shock and grief.

Chapter 17

Kate answered the door, and without a word walked back into the room leaving the door ajar for her parents to enter.

"You didn't even have the decency to call us!" her mother howled. "Scott lying near death in some hospital . . ."

Her mother, choking on emotion, dabbed at her eyes with a handkerchief. ". . . and the police calling. Asking sick questions. And then the reporters . . ." Her mother's grief turned into a shriek. "Do you know what they told us? Do you know what we've been through? Do you?"

Kate looked at her mother: shrunken prematurely, a shriveled witch, an evil presence more real as an adult than she could have ever been to the mind of a child. Anger ripped through Kate's depression, gathered in her eyes, diminished the anguish in her mind.

Her mother waited for an answer. Calmly Kate replied, "Scott was a rapist who terrorized this city for months —"

"No!" her mother shouted at her.

"Yes!" Kate replied in a strong even voice.

"Now, Kate," her father broke in. "That's not a fact."

"It's as much a fact as anything my scientific background prepares me to accept as fact," Kate answered quickly. "The police found journals up in his room. Fibers from his clothes to match those left at rape scenes. More importantly, he turned on his own family — I shot him when he tried to attack either me — or the woman who is renting the cottage out back —"

"And this woman is a known homosexual — a perversion of nature — renting our cottage!" Her mother raised the pitch of the argument. "Of course, Scott wanted her out —"

"The other women he attacked were not lesbians." Kate felt some of the depression of the week return to her body. Scott was a mental basket case and, yes, she had shot him. That was awful enough. Almost more than she could deal with. But the press had had to play up Angie's lesbianism. RIVER RAPIST SHOT BY SISTER was the story of the year in Sacramento — with all of its details carving like a blunt rusty knife into the flesh of her private life. The story had even made the national wire services. She had found the courage to say that Angie was a close personal friend. She had not found the courage to say to the press or to anyone who looked questioningly at

171

her that Angie was her lover. She didn't know how to separate out the issues; to deal with Scott's mental problems, the associated guilt of her family connection, and her recently admitted sexuality. It was more than she could take in emotionally.

"It's a frame, don't you see?" her father pleaded. "They needed someone to pin this on. Scott was only trying to get that sick woman off his property. Our property —"

"No." Kate would not allow this fiction. "You did this to Scott. Both of you. I don't know how or why. But Scott is free now. His journals are not the writings of a sane person. His mind is gone. God knows how long he's been in this condition. But he's my brother, and I hurt." Kate massaged her chest and swallowed the tears. "You've been to the hospital?"

"He's just in shock," her mother said. "His own sister shooting him —"

"I also saved his life. If someone else had caught him, he could be dead."

"He's an innocent baby!" her mother shouted.

"He was a tortured man. And as far as I'm concerned, you murdered him years ago —"

Kate felt the palm of her mother's hand strike her cheek, and with the swift reflexes of an athlete, struck back — not in anger, but by instinct.

Her mother staggered backward. Her father grabbed Kate's arm.

"Get your hand off me," Kate commanded, staring into his face.

He dropped her arm and looked down at his feet.

"You must move to Florida now," Kate's mother said.

"What!" Amazement filled Kate's voice.

"We've put this house up for sale," her father mumbled down at his shoes.

"You must live with us. We'll take Scott home, and you must tend him. Families take care of their own."

Kate's vision blurred. Amazement still in her voice, she uttered, "I went into medicine to heal wounds ... but the ones in this family are utterly terminal. You have no concept of what Scott has done. He'll either end up in a mental hospital or jail. Florida?" Kate held up a hand to her mother who was trying to interrupt. "The fact that we share the same planet is a closeness too near for me. You take the money from the house and go back to Florida. I'll go in the opposite direction."

"We'll cut you out of our will!" her mother shouted.

"You're not listening to me," Kate shouted back. "I want nothing to do with you! I don't want your money. I don't want you in my life. I don't want you near me. I hope you have a place to stay tonight, because you're not staying here!"

Deliberately, coldly, Kate surveyed both her parents. Her mother looked martyred and righteous and small. Her father again hung his head, his mouth a constipated grimace, his eyes dead. He too looked small. They were only mortal after all.

Her stare locked with her mother's. Her mother looked away, then down. Then for a fleeting second, her mother's eyes came back up to hers. Kate knew instantly that she had passed on to her mother years of misplaced guilt and responsibility, and had received back the power she had once abdicated. Her father had removed himself years before. He had imposed his fantasy on a child's body, had had power over the small and the trusting and the silent; and now, having assumed the shape of his fantasy, with no child to molest, he could not live in an adult world. He lived isolated; they were both beyond reach. Scott, equally beyond reach, was the sacrificial repository for all the family's madness — the price exacted for things out of balance.

Her mother's nostrils flared. "You don't know what we've been through!" she screeched.

Rage exploded in Kate's head with the suddenness of fuel combustion, sending shards of adrenalin leaping through her body. She shook. "What *you've* been through! *You?* I have to put my life back together! I have to rise above this and I don't know how! You . . ."

Kate's father stepped toward her. She shoved him back and toward the door. He put up a hand, and she pushed him again.

Angie, a cup of coffee in hand, sat in the cottage. With her free hand, she stroked Sophie's head. She knew Kate's parents were at the main house; she had driven into the driveway as they drove up. She had not seen Kate — not since two nights ago when Kate said she wanted to be left alone.

Angie had no words with which to fight. She felt nearly as devastated over Scott as Kate did. Or maybe she had only taken on Kate's devastation. Vaguely she felt that there was a dark side to all this that her nature couldn't penetrate. It was something that didn't belong to her. But she did feel Kate's loss, and her own depression was as heavy as a black pit.

In some way she also felt responsible. Maybe it was buying the gun. Maybe it was moving into the cottage. Somehow Kate would have been better off if she hadn't been in her life. Certainly the press had mentioned more than once that Angie was a known lesbian — her writing for the gay presses coming back to haunt her.

She had gone back to work for only one day. She couldn't bear the faces that looked the other way when she walked by. But mostly she couldn't face Kate who never once looked at her directly. She didn't know why Kate couldn't look at her. The only explanation she could come up with was that Kate didn't want to be seen with a known lesbian, didn't want that image of herself reflected back in Angie's eyes.

Terry had called yesterday. Angie had spent last night sleeplessly rocking in Terry's arms. Terry had had the good grace not to mention that this could have been avoided had Angie kept her love life in the family. Instead, Terry had reassured her about Kate's love. Advised her to be patient. Told her Kate was a good woman who was going through hard times.

Angie sipped her coffee and felt helpless. She thought back seventeen years to when she was a senior at Berkeley. That had been the year of Jill. Jill and she had been friends for two years before they moved off-campus together. Shortly after that they had been arrested in a large war protest; it had been four in the morning before friends posted bail. Back in their flat, alone, they had fallen into each other's arms, euphorically self-righteous in their mutual martyrdom, aflame with revolutionary zeal. Change, after all, came about only by those willing to break the law. Once in each other's arms, giddy with success, they broke another social taboo. At least that had been true for Jill. She was a born revolutionary. But Angie had had to admit that what she'd wanted all the time was Jill in her arms. It was Jill who had fired her political motivation, not the movement itself.Once she went to bed with Jill they would be crusaders together,

175

committed first to each other and then the Cause. But Jill's sexuality was stirred by political rhetoric alone. After their night of love they had gone to another meeting where they were touted by their comrades. Jill had left with the man who toasted her with the most eloquence. Angie had gone back to the flat alone, in agony. She had finally moved out.

Over the distance of seventeen years, Angie smiled back at her young self. She had known from the first time she touched a girlfriend at a slumber party that she was a lesbian. She hadn't known there was a name for it then. When she was twelve and someone had explained the word "queer" to her, she'd felt relieved — there was a name for what she felt even if, as she learned within seconds, the term was pejorative. Mama, of course, wouldn't talk about it. So Angie had enjoyed the slumber parties, and gone off to Berkeley with most of her innocence in place.

Jill had shattered her naivete — made Angie realize that she wanted more than what women gave each other after they had given the best of themselves to men. She discovered the bars and acquired a lifestyle: A tradition of struggle, of groping toward an ideal, of compromise and pain that gays the world over mitigated through self-deprecating humor, an arrogance of creative style, and nights of intense love. She accepted society's ostracism as the price of individuality and love, and buried herself in history books which after all glorified rebellion and differentness. She had accepted her back-stage hospital role as a way of not drawing attention to herself, as a means of appeasing the social gods. But now she found herself in the spotlight, her lesbianism a front page news item, her way of life a liability to the woman she loved most.

Coffee in hand, she felt the full weight of her personal history. Having outside events control her life, ripped apart by longing for a woman — and waiting. Just as she had always done. She had to question one more time the wisdom of her love. A part of her said she had not chosen well in Kate. Kate was not a sister who had been tested by fire. Angie's own vulnerability left her feeling strangely humiliated. Her normal inclination,to tell the reporters to fuck off, was blocked by her fear of further exposing Kate to this embarrassment. Her militancy might drive Kate further away. She didn't know how to be true to her love for Kate and at the same time be true to herself. She knew, as every woman who ever confronted this conflict, that ultimately her only choice was to be true to herself.

There was a tap at the front door. Angie felt her pulse race as she got up, opened the door.

"May I come in?" Kate looked at her seriously.

"Of course." Angie reached for her hand and led her to the couch. "Your parents?"

"Yes. In their own way, they're crazier than Scott."

"Are they staying in the house?"

"Oh, no. They're out." Absolute certainty resided in Kate's voice.

For the first time in a week, Kate turned and looked fully at Angie. Angie did not look away or speak.

"Everything inside me wants to run away — from you, from this house, from work." Kate looked down at Sophie, rubbed her head.

"That's an option." Angie didn't want to sound cold, but she was fighting the panic that Kate's words brought forth. Irrationally she said, "You have a marathon to run in three weeks."

"I can't even run across the street." Kate shook her head.

177

Angie felt her love for Kate overcome her own fear and pain. She reached across the couch for Kate's hand. "Honey, what can I do for you?"

Kate shook her head. "I don't know."

She looked at Angie, and Angie saw the tears on her cheeks. "Can I spend the night here?" Kate asked.

"Under any circumstances, you can spend the night here. I want you. I want to hold you."

"Angie, I need your fire, your strength. I know I've shut you out most of this week. I'm sorry. I'm confused. I don't know what to do. Forgive me."

"Katie, I don't know if you want me in your life or if you don't. I can accept either. But I need to know."

"I can't answer you right now," Kate whispered and put her head in her hands. "I don't even know if I'm worth having. I don't like myself at this moment. I feel need. I don't feel love." She looked over at Angie.

Angie read clearly all the pain in Kate's eyes. "Okay." Angie nodded, accepting this answer for the moment. "Because I know that I am, I know that you too are infinitely worth having."

"No!" Kate shouted. "You don't know that!"

Suddenly Kate threw her arms back, lifted her head and screamed. Just as quickly she turned on Angie, urgently gripping the back of her head, forcing her mouth onto Angie's.

Angie just as quickly threw Kate off, and stood up, breathlessly confronting her.

"If you want to fight, we'll fight! But I won't make love to you like this. Now or ever!"

In silence they looked at each other. Angie walked over to Kate, and knelt in front of her. She took Kate's hands, and in an offering of trust, placed her head in

Kate's lap. She felt Kate shaking. Moving next to her, Angie took Kate in her arms.

Over the last months, she had seen Kate cry, had comforted her. But this was much more immense. Angie felt as though she were holding all the despair in the universe, and in Kate's moaning, all the dark and ugly creatures residing in her belly spilt out through her mouth, emptied into the room. The creatures did not frighten Angie. She held Kate firmly, and knew, just as firmly, that when the darkness and ugliness were out, light and love would enter.

Chapter 18

Thanksgiving morning. Angie placed the breakfast tray on the bed, sat down. For the last week and a half, whenever she wanted to talk with Kate, it was to the bed she came. As far as she knew, Kate got up to go to work, and had gotten up once to run. For the rest, she came home and went to bed, staring for hours at the ceiling so that Angie herself now addressed the ceiling when talking with her.

"Come on, Kate, *mangia.* You need to eat." The spicy odor of sausage mingled with the sharp scent of coffee. "You're a runner with a race to run."

"Think so?" Kate looked at the breakfast tray, reached for the coffee.

"No, Kate!" Angie whispered in exaggerated exasperation, shaking her head. "Don't you know anything about Thanksgiving breakfast? First the orange juice, then the bearclaw and then the coffee."

"I see." Kate smiled as she accepted the orange juice.

"Now, Katie, can we pretend that your mouth is an airplane hanger, and I'm going to take this little B-52 and glide it right into the hanger?" Angie piled a spoon full of egg, and started it off in the direction of Kate's mouth. "Come on, open."

"Okay," Kate giggled. "Just give me the plate. I'll eat it all. Promise."

Angie smiled, content. She hadn't heard Kate giggle in weeks.

Leaning back against the pillow, Kate drank her coffee. "I missed you." She looked at Angie.

Angie had spent three days in Berkeley and had only returned late last night. "Did you?" Angie felt her heart lurch. "I guess I need to hear things like that. I didn't get much work done. Thought mostly. Walked around."

"I've been a drain on you," Kate acknowledged.

"I just needed time away. It's not you or me. Just the circumstances. I can't keep working at the hospital. I can't take in anymore — it's not a reflection of who I am or what I want. I needed to think about what to do."

"A time for change for me too." Kate finished her breakfast and tested the warmth of her coffee. It was perfect.

"And I'm concerned about you and me," Angie admitted.

"We've been fighting a lot, but it's important to me, Angie. I've never been able to fight with anyone. I walk away." Kate rested her head on a pillow, and sighed. Angie waited for her to go on.

"I don't have words to thank you, I don't know how ... you don't walk out in a fight. You fight with me and then you hold me and tell me it's okay. You're teaching me it's not the end of the world to be angry."

"Oh, fighting is okay with me," Angie said with a laugh. "My problem is not saying more than I mean to say ... to not be hurtful. You know, with all my brothers and sisters, you just yelled the most hurtful thing you could think of at the top of your lungs. It was volume that counted. I guess because softness is so much a part of your nature, you're teaching me tenderness in fighting. But —" Angie turned to Kate, "Fighting isn't really a part of your nature, is it?"

"Not with other people, sweetie."

"Then I'm flattered that you've been yelling back at me." Angie smiled. "I was afraid it meant that you wanted to push me away."

"No, I don't want to push you away," Kate took Angie's hand and squeezed. Putting her coffee down, Kate took Angie into her arms. "Please make love with me."

In answer, Angie took Kate's mouth to hers, and ran her hand lightly from Kate's knee up to her thigh while at the same time her soul slid gently along Kate's flesh seeking entrance to her heart.

As the women stood in a semi-circle behind the piano singing, Kate looked around the living room. The house was as beautiful as the voices now filling it, the voices a reflection of external harmony. Angie had filled her in on the drive over to Terry's and Peg's about the women who would be here; but the smell of dinner cooking, the comfort of the home, and the warmth of the women around the piano was not something she had actually anticipated.

While still singing, the women had greeted Angie with pats on the shoulder or smiles broad enough to span an ocean. They pulled Angie into the circle, and Angie in turn pulled Kate.

The woman next to Kate leaned close to her ear, and with an easy familiarity said, "I'm Peg — Terry's partner. Did you get to leave your beeper at home?"

"No." Kate shook her head, remembering that Peg was a surgeon in another hospital. "Are you on call too?"

Peg nodded. "Um. The luck of the draw. But not to worry. Half the women here are either doctors or counselors. The first called doesn't have to do dishes. The rest have to come back at four in the morning and clean up."

Kate laughed and relaxed. She felt as if she had walked into her own element, only without the hard, competitive cynical edges. She realized instantly that the love given Angie by this group was also extended to her in genuine open-heartedness.

The women finished their own rendition of "Sweet Adeline" and, amid calls for other songs, Terry shouted that she needed three to help in the kitchen. Kate motioned to Angie that she would help. Rather than follow her, Angie allowed Kate to go off alone. If Angie had any wish, it was that Kate would find her own way in this group, find her own niche. When Peg followed Kate into the kitchen, and then Marty, another doctor, trailed off as well, Angie laughed to herself. Leave it to the three medical doctors to gather around one another. But with Terry in the kitchen to direct, dinner was safe.

The music in the living room blended with the laughter in the kitchen. Warmth from the fireplace mixed with turkey and gravy and cinnamon-scented air. Angie was glad she had come back to Sacramento for Thanksgiving — this was home. Her friends in Berkeley, though good company, were not immediate family. More than that, she was happy to be sharing this with Kate who initially had said she wouldn't come. Only after making love with Angie this morning had Kate agreed to dinner — not because she wanted to go out, but because she wanted to stay physically close to Angie.

Glenda, standing next to Angie, put her strong arm around Angie's shoulder and asked in reference to Kate, "How's she doing?"

"I think she'll be okay." Angie nodded, appreciating the ready concern of her friend. Kate would do well here. Perhaps, Angie reflected, too well. This gathering could not be a substitute for the race Kate must run. The family could help you heal, but it could not do the healing. Kate must run her race.

"Nice looking lady." Anita, her brown eyes sparkling, winked across the circle at Angie. "You going to let this woman join the sisterhood and not keep her home in bed?"

"I would like that." Angie laughed, knowing the reference was to Rochelle who she had never once considered bringing into the family. Kate was family. Rochelle was not.

"Good. She has great vibes." Glenda's white teeth showed approval.

184

Yolanda stopped singing long enough to offer, "That wasn't the first thing *I* noticed about her but . . ."

"Now really!" broad-shouldered Linda yelled above the singing, "how can you tell the color of a woman's nipples through a dark sweater? Tell us that, Yollie."

The group roared its delight, everyone by now knowing Yolanda's explicit sexual preferences.

Angie squeezed Sharon's shoulder when Terry announced dinner. "I'll race you to the dining room."

"Lena —" Sharon's happy face smiled up from the wheelchair. "In your excitement you'd probably fall and hurt yourself. The cooler head has the advantage here." Sharon quickly maneuvered her wheels, blocking Angie, and raced off to the dining room.

Angie looked for Kate, who was talking with Peg. Their eyes met; Kate's eyes spoke silently of a contentment that flowed the length of her relaxed posture. Angie took her hand while ruffling Peg's hair. "Mind if I cut in?" Angie addressed both women.

"This is a nice woman." Peg, her long brown hair shining in the candlelight, turned back to Kate, "I want to see more of you."

Kate smiled her acceptance of this invitation even as Angie directly addressed Peg, "You can see more of her a week from this Sunday. The International Marathon. Kate wants to qualify for the Olympic time trials. Why don't you and Terry come out and cheer this woman on?"

Peg's eyes widened. "I'm impressed. Of course we'll come."

As Peg turned to the group, Kate squeezed Angie's hand in anger, and mumbled, "Damn you."

The necessity to answer was cut off as Peg addressed the group: "Okay everyone. A slight departure from ritual this year. I want everyone to remain *standing* while Judy

185

does the "Praise Goddess" piece on the flute. And remain standing while Susan does the blessing. Then we'll sit down and do the toasting. Got it?"

Everyone nodded, and one brave soul asked why.

"Because —" Peg raised her eyebrows to the group. "Half of you nibble through the ceremonies when we sit down first."

"Oh, I see." The rotund Anita looked around the group. "This is personal."

The women laughed, and Terry, with a smile that embraced everyone in the room, invited the women to join hands.

Chapter 19

On the first Sunday of December Kate stood behind the starting line of the Sacramento International Marathon. She was about five feet from the front, in the area designated for those who intended to run six minute miles. It required no effort to close out the excitement of the people around her. She noted absently George McGuire head-to-head with Janet Swan, a young woman he was coaching for the Olympics. Also in the area were two other elite runners from the east. Michelle Downs, denizen of the running arena for years, was clearly here for the money — a ten thousand dollar purse for the first place man and woman, three thousand for each division winner. Kate knew the AAU rules; even if she won her division, she would not accept the money.

But Kate felt detached, uninterested in the race. She was here simply because Angie had placed her in a pair of running shorts, had led her to the car, had driven her to this place.

She looked back to that day in May when she had decided to commit herself to this goal. She might not have been wildly happy at that time — certainly she had been bored with her life. It had been a time of questioning her values, a time of self-examination, a time of discontent. But, and she tried to remember this honestly, her life had been stable, well-ordered; full of promise that somehow now seemed far off and nebulous.

She deeply understood that running a marathon was a commitment undertaken only by those who had their lives in order or, not having their lives in order, were willing to suppress the loose ends. A marathoner had to have time to train — without distractions. A marathoner needed a certain comfort level in terms of money if only to accommodate the added expense of groceries and a doctor bill or two for stress-related injuries. A marathoner didn't have the energy to clean the house or mow the yard. Everything in life took a back seat. The race was everything.

People starving to death in Africa didn't train for marathons — living was challenge enough. Even the average American, under daily stress, would never dream of expending the effort required. Only the fittest of the leisure class could afford the arrogance of long distance running; an arrogance that minimally assumed today was perfect and tomorrow would be better.

How naive she had been! How confident! What she had felt was the freshness of all beginnings. That, and the implicit promise that if you followed the rules, did things according to the books, if you ran your weekly miles and ate properly, then everything would happen the way you had planned. Wasn't this the immutable contract one had with the universe? If your knowledge was correct, and your application impeccable — then you won. Now it was apparent that Angie's theory of randomness had as much to do with winning as anything else. Jokers were passed out in this card game. Or mysterious spices imported from a strange land were sprinkled haphazardly into a giant cauldron altering irrevocably the recipe one lived by. The universe promised nothing.

The starting gun went off. Kate automatically pressed the timing mode on her watch, and set out.

Stick with your commitment — run the marathon, Angie had said. Sure. Easy for Angie to say. Had Angie ever done anything that stretched her limits? Without effort or thought Angie paced herself perfectly through life — never winning big, but never losing either unless the loss could somehow be reinvented as a plus. Angie had a knack for living.

Bitterly, Kate thought back to Angie's words: "You don't heal by lying in bed with the covers up over your head." Really? Kate knew she had always picked herself up without complaining and continued. Nothing had ever kept her down, not her, not Kate Ashbourne. But look where it had gotten her. She had played by all the rules — and shot her own brother, a demented rapist! Her life was tainted by some genetic sickness.

"Oedipus slept with his mother," Angie had said during one of their arguments.

"He didn't know it was his mother," Kate had replied.

"You didn't know you were shooting your brother."

"But I sure as hell knew it was my father who cornered me in the bedroom. The whole family is sick!"

"Kate, you had no choice with your father. That was a question of power and betrayal. Your *father* is sick, not you!"

"You're missing the point," Kate yelled back. "It's fate. It's in the genes. What if I'd had children?"

"So Cain killed Abel. History's a repeated refinement of genocide. Good people die young and in ugly ways but we still go on having children, believing the good outweighs the bad. This is part of being human, it's not personal."

"That's no consolation, Mandelli!" Kate shouted. "I don't see you out there having children. Maybe your kind of sterility is the best that can be hoped for."

"Hey!" With shaking hands, Angie grabbed at her. "You're not dragging me into this sickness you see. Don't you dare! You know what I think?"

Kate shook her head, not wanting to hear anything more of what Angie thought.

"I think you're not really committed to yourself. You couldn't commit to your work or to Alex or to anyone who was ever in your life. I'm a diversion. The commitment you ultimately lack is to your own life. You run marathons just to see if you're still alive or only pretending. The physical pain is real. And if you didn't have your miles to think about when you wake up in the morning, you might have to confront real and even more painful psychological issues — like who the person is that's getting out of bed. The only thing lacking in your life, Katie, is you!"

"Just answer me this." Kate had catapulted from the bed on which they sat. "Did Oedipus have a long and happy life?"

"Fuck Oedipus! We're not living a goddam Greek tragedy!" Angie had jumped off the bed, following Kate. "This is real life! You lay down and die from the sadness of it or you get up and go on! Where are your guts, woman?"

The mile timer called out six-five. Kate looked down at her watch. She was running too fast.

Sure, she thought, either you get up and go on or lay down and die. But the choices are never that simple. Most people did get up. People did go on. But at what price? The ambulatory crippled out there — hiding disabilities, limping around with crutches propping up their hearts, or their minds already locked away in a private asylum: remote, unreachable, unknowing and unknown.

Her brother. What crippling event did he dust off himself, then get up and go on? His hidden wound festering, gathering puss, ulcerating underneath tan healthy skin. Her father? A terminal, spiritual tumor. Her mother? Probably she had her own set of scars ready to break the permanence of their stitching, spilling out an intestinal miasma.

So why should she slow down now? Go for broke, that would be better. Die crossing the finish line. Slow down. Speed up. Makes no difference in the end. Obey the rules. Disregard them. No difference. We're all the same six feet under. Why, as a doctor, had she never realized this? Because, she told herself, we concentrate on relieving the pain. Really? Is that why we dole out morphine in controlled doses to dying patients? Is that why we drag the dead back to life and pride ourselves that those paralyzed from the neck down are still breathing? No. We fight death and fail to notice that we've lost before we start. Pain is what we *should* concentrate on.

Lost in thought, Kate didn't hear the two mile time. She was recalling Mona, a hospital colleague and friend. Mona had initially gone into hospice work, and over coffee one day, tired from night rotation, she had talked about a patient in coma for ten years. The stress on the family — the husband had been coming to the hospice every day for ten years. Mona had pulled the plug on her patient, and then lived with the fear that the cleaning personnel would notice and report her to staff. "Doctors don't do this," Mona had whispered, and Kate saw her chin quiver, her eyes moist over. So that's why Mona had stopped doing hospice work, Kate remembered thinking, slightly embarrassed over Mona's tears, not knowing what to do or say. Now she realized that Mona had made a decision to treat the family pain rather than continue the battle with death. She had gone against her professional ethics, done a human thing rather than a doctor thing.

I will get out of radiology and take up a general practice, Kate promised herself. She looked at her watch and suddenly realized that her body felt good.

So she had missed three weeks of training. Maybe staying in bed was not the wisest thing — her body was trained to run, and she knew the importance of exercise for the depressed mind. That knowledge had not gotten her up. But on the other hand, her body was now rested, her legs doing what her mind could not; moving forward powerfully, ahead of pace, doing what they were trained to do.

A new thought struck her: Maybe that was the problem — she hadn't been doing what she was trained to do. She was trained to relieve pain; to cure the symptoms when knowledge allowed, but to always make the patient feel better. Forget professional ethics, forget the battle with death. Maybe that was the wisdom of country doctors — they took themselves out of big hospital politics and all of its restrictions so that they could better serve people. She could do that too. Instead of sitting at a desk and reading symptoms twice removed. She was a practicing technician when what she was trained to do — what she really wanted to do — was heal people. She hadn't been utilizing her talents. Forty-two, and she was out here running a marathon, avoiding the real game she was fully trained to play.

Game? she questioned herself as she reached for a cup of water on the water table. Well, yes, amateur athletics had a lot to be said for it. Discipline, character, strength. All those things applied to living as much as to a game. She smiled ruefully. Platitudes. Taught at the Big Ten and Ivy League universities. They slip the quarterback jock a Cadillac under the table and touch up his grades. This is character building?

Okay. Is there a difference between living and playing? Coaches didn't think so. She thought back to Ben Estes, her high school coach, a small wiry man, fanatically serious. "Run! Faster! For the glory of Encina High, girls!" Somehow, in all the running, individuality got lost. Yes, she remembered, that was it. She had taken up running because out on the track, in a unified form of movement, she forgot all the problems at home — forgot her father. Got lost in the effort. Sure Encina was covered with glory. Sure, she had become a national champ. But the thrill of the game was in self-forgetfulness — hard-working teammates, all playing fast, playing to win, buoyed to an elevation above self.

Could life, like a game, be played that way?

Was it possible to lose oneself in the effort of living in order to win? Was that how things worked? Like the football player who hurls his body into the line, without thought of personal injury, could one give it all up on the playing field of life for the greater glory of all? Oh, sure, the football player got paid for it. But at the moment he committed his body, he wasn't thinking that his million dollar contract was worth crippled legs; he was lost in the game. Like she got lost in running. Or was this kind of self-forgetfulness desirable? *What* did the jock do when he was crippled for life at twenty-five? What new game did the joker deal him?

The five mile time was called — thirty minutes and five seconds. With all her thinking, she had lost four miles, and was ahead of her pace. but she wasn't breathing hard. The pace was easy. She could run like this forever. For the first time she noticed that the day was overcast — perfect for running.

A thread of conversation wove its way into her mind. Angie sitting in the car, driving to the start of the race. She had noted the weather, commented on the cool conditions. Kate couldn't remember her own answer. An automatic response probably. Angie, Kate thought. If life was like a team sport, Angie was the perfect teammate. Even in the last three terrible weeks Angie had acted in every way supportive; had teased her, shouted at her, made her show up for the race, had held her to her commitment. Oh, yes, there were times when Angie could drive you crazy, but those were like time-out periods. If your team was losing and needed something to laugh about, Angie was not beyond playing the clown. But in the game itself, Angie was a team player — smart, committed, unflagging in her energy. Okay, Ashbourne, let's drop the analogy. Platitudes. A jock with platitudes. Angie deserved better.

The stillness of the Sunday morning crept into Kate's consciousness, together with the flap-flap of her running shoes on the pavement. Kate looked around, for the first time feeling oriented to the day and the race. There was a pack of eight men running about two hundred feet ahead. The trees along Fair Oaks Boulevard glistened with moisture. The gray clouds above, having poured down rain the day before, seemed to be breaking up. Her reflection came back to her in pools of water along the road; the smile she saw reflected blended with the swoop of a tall pine tree. Could she really be the smile in the puddles? Despite circumstances and pain, could one be happy?

She ran into the day — her quadriceps an extension of the light breeze that carried them forward, her arms and chest lifted by the air that enveloped her. She felt no separation between body and elements. All was lightness and harmony.

A segment of a poem from college came back to her: "Where the pure too-little incomprehensibility changes — springs round into that empty too-much." The self-forgetfulness of language passed into the self-forgetfulness of the race, and what remained was the regular succession of flap-flap, a rhythmical peace like that which poetry guaranteed to the soul.

That was it! In the silence Kate felt elation. The clutter of self-remembering prevented the soul from entering with others into that "empty too-much." The "empty too-much," perhaps frightening for most people, required that you know yourself. You couldn't give up into the "empty too-much" what you didn't know. Loneliness and confusion were the price of unintentional self-forgetting. But to consciously choose surrender was to enter with others into a peaceful void — out of which true creation might flow.

Rilke, Kate placed the poet. Well, God knows she never understood what he was saying twenty-two years ago. But he did make sense now. Flap-flap.

She didn't check the time at six miles — in full stride, time meant nothing.

Okay, she spoke to herself, what can I do? I've spent a month feeling sorry for myself. Depressed, yes, and rightfully so, but what are the options now? Even as this thought passed through her, she realized that the depression had totally lifted. Her body, the neurotransmitters and the endorphines and all the chemistry that made medicine an adventure into magic, buoyed her mind, carried her heart, reaffirmed her commitment — damn Angie, yes, her commitment! — to doctoring.

She would quit her job. She smiled. Radiology was fit only for recluses. She would become a general practitioner. She would join the front line of those people her ancient profession had prepared her to be among. Would Angie move with her to some small northern California town? She dare not make the same mistake as Alex and assume Angie would automatically go. Besides, she would need another year of med school to refresh her skills.

More schooling would be no problem. Frugal and conservative, she had accumulated a good deal of money. Unlike Angie, she never bought without necessity breathing hard down her back. Even a new dress was something she begrudgingly considered only after realizing she had worn the same one around the same group of people far too often. Jewelry meant little to her.

The house she and Scott lived in was paid for — they had only paid taxes. So her parents were selling it? She had done all the tax shelter seminars the hospital offered its doctors, and had made good investments in commercial real estate. Buying a house right now didn't interest her, but something small might make more sense than renting. She would talk it over with Angie.

As the seven mile keeper called out 42:10, a thought clung to Kate's mind. She and Scott would no longer be sharing a house. Scott would never be living with her again. As she tried to recall the exact last conversation she had had with him, tears welled in her eyes, but her legs ran on. Pizza. The same night he had broken into the cottage, he had yelled down the hall to her and Angie asking if they wanted pizza. There was no place to put these thoughts.

What had Angie said several weeks ago? "Reality is only reality — not easy or hard. Those are judgments we make about it in our minds."

"Oh, for chrissake!" she had retorted. "What does that mean?"

"The truth is, some of it is fun and some of it isn't. You can feel it. Laugh or cry over it. Ultimately reality is a perception of the heart."

"I don't know what you're talking about." Kate had turned her face away.

"Of course you don't." Angie had pulled Kate's face back. "You've got a ten foot wall — six feet thick — around your heart."

"What do you think I feel for you, then, Ms. Mandelli?"

"Lust, Katie, lust. Erotica is emotionally cheap. It's very mental."

197

Kate heard the eight mile time called out from a vast distance. Through tears she looked down at her watch, and saw only blurring digits.

She had never known her brother. She would have died for him; instead she had shot him. He had never known her. She felt sure he would have risked his life for her too. They were all the family each other had. Through circumstances neither controlled, they had turned on each other.

She, a doctor, hadn't even recognized that Scott had been sick. Whatever torment had deformed his mind, Scott had needed help. And she hadn't known that — had taken him and his health for granted, had hidden behind the wall of her heart, and not truly allowed him in. Angie was right. She read X rays, not people. The emotional expenditure was too great. Now that it was too late to save Scott, she recognized that emotional expenditure was required to live fully. This lesson was not fair. Flap-flap.

She reached the nine mile mark. Tears flooded the sweat on her face. She felt utterly alone. Her legs moved forward, on pace.

"What do you think?" she had shouted at Angie. "Tears make everything better? If we just had more collective crying, the holocaust would be atoned for?"

"No." Angie had grabbed her shoulder. "I think if we could connect with the tears inside us the holocaust would never have happened. Tears are the ocean that sustains us."

At ten miles she heard her time called out at one hour exactly. She came out of herself and looked at her watch. She had been running too fast — six minute miles. In depression, in exuberance, and then in pain, she had lost all sense of pace. This was not the way to run a race. Or was it?

She thought back to the first marathon she had run five years ago. What had she been looking for then? After college, she'd kept up her running. But only short distances, five or six miles. The exercise kept her fit. She read her track and field magazines, and did keep up on other runners.

Then something in an article she read had hooked her: The notion that a marathon was a microcosm of life, that most western people never had the opportunity to test their courage or the limits of their pain or the boundaries of their will. Western life valued compromise and conformity. These values, adhered to without exception or question, could lead to a kind of self-deception and collective frustration. But alone with yourself for twenty-six miles, you couldn't lie. When your mind finally broke down — shouted at you to stop, and you kept on running by virtue of your will, then you came to know a power not even remotely related to a personal ego. You came to know yourself face to face.

In the first marathon she had run the issue for her was pain. Angie was right in a way — in that accusation about avoiding pain. During the years of dealing with her father, she had constructed that wall around her heart — the one that kept away all pain. Oh, yes, she had always pushed herself, but even in track, the push had only been to the threshold of pain. A marathon was different. You had to enter the pain at some point, and you had to be mindful that at any moment a ligament could go, a bone could stress to fracture. Just as importantly there was the voice in the head, the voice that came on at twenty miles, and reminded you that you were on the brink of death. If you tried to ignore the voice or if you tried to answer it, it got hysterical and screamed. The trick, she had learned in that first marathon, was in patient listening — not to answer, not to ignore, but to hear and love and keep on running. Flap-flap.

At eleven miles she felt strong.

Yes, her father. So did you only transcend pain in a race? How did you transcend emotional pain? Prayer. God. Kate looked out at the day. Maybe that too was only a question of mindful listening — without judgment, without answers. Maybe a good God was inside us all. Her left hamstring twitched. She rubbed it.

Her father had been her best friend. Played baseball with her when he came home from work. Talked to her as if she were an adult. Had actually stood up for her sometimes — acts of exceptional courage she had not understood at the time. He was the only person in the world who protected her, to whom she turned for all her deepest needs.

How could she forgive the betrayal? Her therapist had said she would never forget. Forgiveness? How? Yet she had shot her brother. Who would forgive her? Who does the forgiving?

Who does the judging?

As the twelve mile time was called out, the memory of that first marathon came fully back. At sixteen miles she had been consumed with pain. At that point she had asked herself, "Who feels the pain?" The question, so unexpected, silenced her mind, sent the small voice in her head into retreat. Thoughtfully, peacefully, a small voice finally came back, "I don't know. It doesn't matter."

The journey of the race was beyond personality. The answers people sought in boredom failed to be questions when engaged in the running. Flap-flap.

Thirteen miles. One hour, nineteen minutes. Only half way through the race. The hamstring still hurt, but aside from that she felt great. Rationally she understood that this pace was suicidal, but her body told her to run, run.

She looked out again at the day. Billows of gray clouds folded into pure white ones. *The pavilion of Heaven is bare* . . . Shelley, she told herself. *Like a child from the womb, like a ghost from the tomb, I arise and unbuild it again* . . . Are we all capable of death and resurrection? The transmutation of clouds. Kate giggled. English 1A should be a course reserved for forty-two-year-old women. No, she answered herself, I will not teach English. A general practice. Not too near Mendocino. Angie might take it into her head that Sheila was the right woman for her. Flap-flap.

Lust? Angie was right. As long as she kept a fortress around her heart, lust was the only possibility. But Angie didn't understand. Just because the words were never spoken, never seemed good enough . . . well, Angie was inside the fortress, not outside. Angie was at the core of her heart.

At fourteen miles Kate looked at her watch. From this moment I'll do better with my life, she resolved. I can't heal my brother. And I still must deal with the loss of him, of Alex, of all the people I have only allowed partial access to myself. I must heal. I must do more schooling. And move from the house. More pain, surely. Yet I can commit myself now to doing better. That's what the race is about. Doing your best, one foot in front of the other. Moving with the pain, not against it. Flap-flap.

At fifteen miles the hamstring was feeling better. Aha, Kate congratulated herself with humility, it's a pain that can be run through. She smiled and held the day close to her. Alone is not so bad. Alone is not always alone. Like pain and pleasure, like happiness and sadness, alone and together transcends the limits of dichotomy too.

201

Everything finally converges. We swim together, alone or apart, sustained on an ocean of tears — happy tears and sad tears. The empty too-much.

At sixteen miles Kate heard the flap-flap of approaching shoes. She wasn't startled when a voice addressed her.

"Some fun?" the tired voice inquired.

Kate looked at the skinny young man beside her. "You mean you're not having any yet?" she teased, although she still felt strong.

"Been following you all the way." The man's eyes, sunken into a haggard wet face, still sparkled. "I want to finish in under three hours. Never done that before."

"Hey, you look in great shape." Kate stretched the truth to encourage the man. Maybe she could pull him forward a little.

"What's your ETA?" He gave her a wink.

"A pilot, huh? We're going to land around two-forty-five."

"Sounds like a crash landing to me."

"For me too," Kate admitted.

"Just want to thank you. You carried me this far." He paused, and Kate smiled at him. "You look good up close. But you know, you look great from behind. I think I'll follow you some more." He flirted, but Kate was aware of what he was really saying to her.

"Good luck." She maternally reached across the distance, and ruffled his wet head.

The man slowed his pace, and Kate pulled away. She felt as though she left some of her energy with him. That's OK, she assured herself. He needs it.

At seventeen miles Kate started through a physical check. Her right foot. Her left foot. No blisters. Her right ankle. No weakness. For the next two miles she occupied herself in this way — the doctor in her slowly taking inventory. It was an old game. When she came to a sore area she mentally massaged it. She knew that within the last miles of the race she would not possess the clarity to do this.

At twenty miles she checked her time. Given her physical state, her time was too fast. Now the question was how to make it. The hamstring felt good — but it could go at any time. Her hips ached. More importantly, the strength within her was waning. She would have to run the next three miles intelligently, and the last three on will.

She slowed her pace, and put the race out of her mind. Okay, she would heal people — if they wanted to be healed. Sometimes people didn't. Without judgment, you left those people and went on to the people who wanted help. Life was not for judging. It was for service.

She looked out at the day, and hugged it to her. There might not be another day like this one. Suddenly she didn't want the race to end. She wanted to run forever, feeling this time and this place under her feet, within her heart. For the next several miles she looked outside herself, pulling the external day into herself, fixing firmly all details.

Just as suddenly, she slipped into exhaustion. This is where you go on, Ashbourne. This is it. Flap-flap.

At twenty four miles she looked at her watch. This is it; this is survival. One foot in front of the other. Brutal. Survival is carved out in the sweat caked to your face in white sheets of salt. It's carried in the bones that ache for respite. You step on other people and never notice through your own pain. Survival takes the measure of those who didn't survive. It also looks toward those who carry on. You hope they do a better job than you did.

You survive. There is no room for arrogance. You can't say what a fine job you did. You can only say that others, given your ability, would have done the same. Given your need they would have acted the same way. Given your humanity they would have faltered too. No, Angie, life is not a Greek tragedy. It is also not survival of the fittest. It is only survival — humbling and awesome, passed from one generation to the next, all doing the best they can.

Two hundred yards to go. Kate thought of Angie, and what she would tell her. What she would ask of her; what she wanted to know from her. One foot. The next. Flap-flap.

Kate crossed the finish line in two forty-three. A man took her racing number as Angie rushed up with water. Kate bent over and, giving in to the watery feeling in her legs, slid down to the ground. Angie used her own body to soften Kate's descent, and then began to massage her legs. Kate caught her breath, sighed, and felt her body relax in Angie's hands.

"My bags are packed for Eugene, Katie." A smile filled Angie's face, accenting her deep dimples and the creases around her eyes. She stood up. "Let me go get you some more water."

"Wait." Kate touched Angie's shoulder. "I want to tell you something."

Angie sat down nearly in Kate's lap and stared into her eyes. "Okay."

"I may lust after you. I hope I always do. But you know for the last twenty-six miles I've . . ." Kate searched for words.

Angie nodded.

"You've got to know, angel . . . I love life dearly. And I love you as much as life." Kate rested her head back into

204

Angie's lap and looked up into Angie's face. "Stay with me?"

"Of course." Angie swallowed the lump in her throat, and stroked Kate's wet head.

From Angie's lap, Kate looked over to the state capitol steps where other runners shuffled in restless exhaustion, their heads hanging like buttons on ragged clothes. She looked up over the palm trees, and took a deep breath. Her lungs filled with the elevation of a precisely blue expanse of sky, and she held it there inside herself. Finally she expelled the air, and shivered.

"Cold?" Angie quickly covered Kate with a jacket. "More water?"

"Hey!" Kate's eyes glistened as she weakly pulled at a strand of Angie's hair. "Just sit here with me for a minute. I'm claiming my prize."

"Oh, Kate." Angie smiled broadly.

Across the green lawn of Capitol Park a group of women yelled and waved as they came running toward the two women. Peg, her hair flowing, pulled Terry along at the front of the group.

"A cheering section." Kate forced her body into an upright position.

"For you." Angie kissed the back of Kate's head as she massaged her shoulders.

"Yes." Kate reached behind, and hugged Angie to her back. "And for you. And for all of us."

A few of the publications of
THE NAIAD PRESS, INC.
P.O. Box 10543 ● Tallahassee, Florida 32302
Phone (904) 539-9322
Mail orders welcome. Please include 15% postage.

SUNDAY'S CHILD by Joyce Bright. 216 pp. Lesbian athletics, at last the novel about sports.   ISBN 0-941483-12-6 $8.95

WE WALK THE BACK OF THE TIGER by Patricia A. Murphy. 192 pp. Romantic Lesbian novel/beginning women's movement.
ISBN 0-941483-13-4   8.95

OSTEN'S BAY by Zenobia N. Vole. 204 pp. Sizzling adventure romance set on Bonaire.   ISBN 0-941483-15-0   8.95

LESSONS IN MURDER by Claire McNab. 216 pp. 1st in a stylish mystery series.   ISBN 0-941483-14-2   8.95

YELLOWTHROAT by Penny Hayes. 240 pp. Margarita, bandit, kidnaps Julia.   ISBN 0-941483-10-X   8.95

SAPPHISTRY: THE BOOK OF LESBIAN SEXUALITY by Pat Califia. 3d edition, revised. 208 pp.   ISBN 0-941483-24-X   8.95

CHERISHED LOVE by Evelyn Kennedy. 192 pp. Erotic Lesbian love story.   ISBN 0-941483-08-8   8.95

LAST SEPTEMBER by Helen R. Hull. 208 pp. Six stories & a glorious novella.   ISBN 0-941483-09-6   8.95

THE SECRET IN THE BIRD by Camarin Grae. 312 pp. Striking, psychological suspense novel.   ISBN 0-941483-05-3   8.95

TO THE LIGHTNING by Catherine Ennis. 208 pp. Romantic Lesbian 'Robinson Crusoe' adventure.   ISBN 0-941483-06-1   8.95

THE OTHER SIDE OF VENUS by Shirley Verel. 224 pp. Luminous, romantic love story.   ISBN 0-941483-07-X   8.95

DREAMS AND SWORDS by Katherine V. Forrest. 192 pp. Romantic, erotic, imaginative stories.   ISBN 0-941483-03-7   8.95

MEMORY BOARD by Jane Rule. 336 pp. Memorable novel about an aging Lesbian couple.   ISBN 0-941483-02-9   8.95

THE ALWAYS ANONYMOUS BEAST by Lauren Wright Douglas. 224 pp. A Caitlin Reese mystery. First in a series.
ISBN 0-941483-04-5   8.95

SEARCHING FOR SPRING by Patricia A. Murphy. 224 pp. Novel about the recovery of love.   ISBN 0-941483-00-2   8.95

DUSTY'S QUEEN OF HEARTS DINER by Lee Lynch. 240 pp. Romantic blue-collar novel.   ISBN 0-941483-01-0   8.95

PARENTS MATTER by Ann Muller. 240 pp. Parents' relationships with Lesbian daughters and gay sons.
ISBN 0-930044-91-6   9.95

THE PEARLS by Shelley Smith. 176 pp. Passion and fun in the Caribbean sun.
ISBN 0-930044-93-2   7.95

MAGDALENA by Sarah Aldridge. 352 pp. Epic Lesbian novel set on three continents.
ISBN 0-930044-99-1   8.95

THE BLACK AND WHITE OF IT by Ann Allen Shockley. 144 pp. Short stories.
ISBN 0-930044-96-7   7.95

SAY JESUS AND COME TO ME by Ann Allen Shockley. 288 pp. Contemporary romance.
ISBN 0-930044-98-3   8.95

LOVING HER by Ann Allen Shockley. 192 pp. Romantic love story.
ISBN 0-930044-97-5   7.95

MURDER AT THE NIGHTWOOD BAR by Katherine V. Forrest. 240 pp. A Kate Delafield mystery. Second in a series.
ISBN 0-930044-92-4   8.95

ZOE'S BOOK by Gail Pass. 224 pp. Passionate, obsessive love story.
ISBN 0-930044-95-9   7.95

WINGED DANCER by Camarin Grae. 228 pp. Erotic Lesbian adventure story.
ISBN 0-930044-88-6   8.95

PAZ by Camarin Grae. 336 pp. Romantic Lesbian adventurer with the power to change the world.
ISBN 0-930044-89-4   8.95

SOUL SNATCHER by Camarin Grae. 224 pp. A puzzle, an adventure, a mystery — Lesbian romance.
ISBN 0-930044-90-8   8.95

THE LOVE OF GOOD WOMEN by Isabel Miller. 224 pp. Long-awaited new novel by the author of the beloved *Patience and Sarah*.
ISBN 0-930044-81-9   8.95

THE HOUSE AT PELHAM FALLS by Brenda Weathers. 240 pp. Suspenseful Lesbian ghost story.
ISBN 0-930044-79-7   7.95

HOME IN YOUR HANDS by Lee Lynch. 240 pp. More stories from the author of *Old Dyke Tales*.
ISBN 0-930044-80-0   7.95

EACH HAND A MAP by Anita Skeen. 112 pp. Real-life poems that touch us all.
ISBN 0-930044-82-7   6.95

SURPLUS by Sylvia Stevenson. 342 pp. A classic early Lesbian novel.
ISBN 0-930044-78-9   6.95

PEMBROKE PARK by Michelle Martin. 256 pp. Derring-do and daring romance in Regency England.
ISBN 0-930044-77-0   7.95

THE LONG TRAIL by Penny Hayes. 248 pp. Vivid adventures of two women in love in the old west.
ISBN 0-930044-76-2   8.95

HORIZON OF THE HEART by Shelley Smith. 192 pp. Hot romance in summertime New England.
ISBN 0-930044-75-4   7.95

AN EMERGENCE OF GREEN by Katherine V. Forrest. 288 pp. Powerful novel of sexual discovery.
ISBN 0-930044-69-X   8.95